HERE COMES CHARLIE MOON

"Come on," says Charlie hoarsely, dragging her arm and shuffling forward. "You hide up here, behind the curtain over the archway. I'm going to be in the entrance hall."

"It isn't worth it, Charlie. Nobody's here. Nobody's going to come . . . are they?" her voice trails off into a squeak of fright.

CHARLIE MOON AND THE BIG BONANZA BUST-UP

"Mr Dix is acting fishy. Norman said so," said Charlie. And he told her what he had already told Norman, about all he had seen through the port-hole of the lighted cabin the night before.

"He was drawing a picture?" said Ariadne. "I thought he was meant to be an art dealer, not an artist."

THE CHARLIE MOON COLLECTION

Shirley Hughes

RED FOX

A Red Fox Book

Published by Random House Children's Books
20 Vauxhall Bridge Road, London SW1V 2SA

A division of Random House UK Ltd
London Melbourne Sydney Auckland
Johannesburg and agencies throughout the world

1 3 5 7 9 10 8 6 4 2

Here Comes Charlie Moon first published in Great Britain by The Bodley Head 1980, *Charlie Moon and the Big Bonanza Bust-Up* first published in Great Britain by The Bodley Head 1982

This Red Fox edition 1998

Printed and bound in Great Britain by
Cox & Wyman Ltd, Reading, Berkshire

Papers used by Random House UK Limited
are natural, recyclable products made from wood grown in sustainable forests. The manufacturing processes conform to the environmental regulations of the country of origin.

RANDOM HOUSE UK Limited Reg. No. 954009

ISBN 0 09 926699 7

CONTENTS

HERE COMES
CHARLIE MOON

1

Charlie Moon's Auntie runs a joke shop at the seaside. It sells things like comic hats, masks, rubber spiders, fake flowers that squirt water at you unexpectedly, and cushions that squeak when you sit down on them. The narrow shop front faces the sea. "JOKES AND CARNIVAL NOVEL-TIES" it says, and underneath, "Jean Llanechan Jones", which is Charlie's Auntie's name. It's easier to say the middle bit properly if you are Welsh, as she is. You have to spit it out rather than say it.

Charlie himself lives in a big city with his Mum, who is in the hairdressing business. There are no jokes in her shop, only a row of lady customers sitting wired up to domed space-helmet drying machines, cooking slowly to lobster red as they flick through their magazines. Charlie tends to trip over their feet whilst skateboarding through the shop from the back room to the street. They don't like it. It puts them off coming. By the end of the first week of the summer holidays Mum's patience has snapped, and Charlie is off to his Auntie Jean's at Penwyn Bay. He can't take his skateboard because it weighs down the suitcase too much. It's too full already, as Charlie is a smart dresser. He wants to pack four changes

of trousers, his T-shirt with Superman on the front, and his red-and-white cap with the big peak. Also his snorkel and mask in case he wants to do some underwater swimming.

"What do you want to pack all that for?" asks Mum, forcing down the suitcase lid by sitting down on it with all her weight. "You can't see anything under water at Penwyn Bay—it's too muddy."

"I might. There might be a big fish or a seal. One of those got washed up on the beach once. I saw a picture of it in the *Penwyn Bay News*."

"You don't need a mask and a snorkel to look at seals," Mum tells him, but they get packed all the same. "You're to help Auntie Jean with the washing-up, and in the shop if she asks you to," Mum goes on. "And don't forget to make your bed properly instead of just dragging the covers up as you do here. Ariadne's going to be there," she adds.

This is not good news for Charlie. Ariadne is his cousin. She is only two years older than he is but it seems more like five because she is so clever. Not stuck up exactly, but her Dad is a very important man who writes things in the newspapers and she reads a lot of books. Charlie likes a good book too, of course, but his mind

often seems somehow to slide off the page and he finds himself doing something else. He once read a book about a cave-man which was great. He'll read that again all right when he's got time. Ariadne being at Auntie Jean's means that she will be sleeping in the best room at the top of the house which looks out to sea, and will be sitting about reading all the time, or saying things that make people feel uncomfortable. She has two favourite words, one is "pathetic" and the other "typical". (Pretty pathetic and typical to go round with a name like Ariadne, come to that, thinks Charlie privately.)

Still, it isn't bad at Auntie Jean's.

The jokes and carnival novelties are all over the place as usual. Rows of rubbery masks are hanging up behind the counter—not the underwater kind, but funny ones of red-nosed clowns, Frankensteins, gorillas and suchlike. In the passage behind the shop are piles and piles of boxes full of crackers, indoor fireworks, magic sets and squeakers that you blow out at people to make them feel jolly. Not even Auntie Jean knows what is inside some of these boxes. In fact, she has a lot of trouble finding things. She often runs out of things to eat, too. This happens on the first afternoon of Charlie's visit.

"I'll just be popping out for a loaf and some fish fingers for tea," she sings out, climbing into her red coat. "And I might just be dropping in at Mrs Goronwy Lewis's on the way back, just for ten minutes, see. Look after the shop, won't you? Everything's priced, and all you've got to remember is to give the right change out of the till and to be ever so polite to the customers."

"I don't suppose there'll be any," says Ariadne, after Auntie's footsteps have tittupped away up the prom. "There hardly ever are. This shop's going bankrupt, if you ask me."

She stretches out on the old sofa in the back room, with a book and Einstein, the old ginger tom cat, on her stomach. From here, with her head propped up, she can see through the open door along the passage to the shop. Charlie has disappeared. All is very still. The afternoon sun lies quietly on the dusty shop floor, and outside the sea washes gently on the stones. Suddenly a strange moaning is heard. It rises to a louder moan, then to a throaty roar. A shuffling creature on all fours advances down the passage, and a monstrous face covered in green hair appears round the arm of the sofa.

Einstein merely twitches one ear.

"You are *pathetic*," says Ariadne, calmly turning over a page.

Charlie takes off the monster mask which he has borrowed from the shop, and gets up off his hands and knees. He hadn't really hoped that Ariadne would think he was a proper monster, but at least she could have pretended for a bit. It would be more fun than just lying about with a book and not talking to people. He's just about to tell her so, too, when the shop door opens with a loud clang, and in come two boys. They are sandy-haired, piggy-eyed and look as though they might be brothers. Both of them are wearing striped jerseys, hooped like barrels around their wide middles.

"Can I help you?" asks Charlie in his best shop-assistant manner, hands spread out on the counter. Ariadne, still reading, wanders out from the back room.

One of the boys starts to finger some false noses and other small items in the show-case by the shop door. The bigger one asks rudely to see some trick card games like the ones in the window. These are kept on the very top shelf behind the counter, so Charlie fetches the little step-ladder and climbs up to get the box. As soon as he has come down the boy says he has changed his mind and wants to try on a Frankenstein mask. This is even higher

up behind the counter, but after Charlie has had some trouble reaching it the boy decides that it's much too expensive and wants to buy some invisible ink instead. Charlie, sighing deeply and trying hard to remember what Auntie Jean said about being polite to the customers, dives under the counter to find the box of invisible inks. It's dark under there, and a lot of boxes fall out on top of him. Some scuffling and sniggering is going on at the other side of the counter.

"Hey, stop it! Put that back!" shouts Ariadne suddenly.

Charlie pops up his head to receive a jet of water in one eye from a water pistol. As he's shaking the water out of his face, he sees both the boys helping themselves from the show-case. Ariadne is round the counter in a flash, trying to stop them. The show-case starts to wobble, false noses and moustaches fall on the floor and confetti flies about all over the shop. As she leaps forward to steady the case the two boys are off out of the shop door and away up the prom, stuffing stolen packets of stink-bombs into their pockets. Ariadne rushes out after them on to the pavement, white with rage.

"Thieves! Robbers!" she shouts, and, under her breath, *"Typical!"*

"I'll get them!" cries Charlie. "I'm the fastest runner in the world! You stay here and mind the shop, Ariadne, while I go after them!"

And he starts off after the boys, legging it like a stag. He can see their striped back-views bobbing up and down in the distance. They're weaving in and out of the shelters, looking back over their shoulders now and again. They know by now that they are being followed. Under the railings, slithering down the sea-wall on to the beach, round the back of the beach-huts, up the steps, back on to the prom again they run. Charlie comes behind, his hair flopping about all over his scarlet face. He really is a good runner, very light and quick. The two boys are not. They are a lot bigger and heavier than Charlie, and they're already getting puffed.

As he runs Charlie starts to wonder what he'll do if he catches them up. He hadn't thought of this before. Now he remembers that there are two of them and only one of him; he's already a long way from the shop. He wishes he had somebody with him. Even Ariadne would be better than nothing. If only he could see a policeman somewhere . . . but they all seem to have gone home for tea.

Now the boys have dodged completely out of sight.

Charlie, cautious and puzzled, pants on. Suddenly, both of them pop out from behind a shelter, grinning right in his path. Charlie stops short. They all face one another. Then . . . . *crack! crack! crack!* Three stink-bombs explode on the ground. Charlie reels back, holding his nose, as the boys disappear up a side road, whistling and jeering. He is left standing there helplessly as the evil-smelling cloud rises about him. At this moment two ladies, one large and the other small, appear as though by magic from the other end of the shelter. They both have handkerchiefs pressed to their noses.

"Whatever's that awful . . . ?" begins one, but the small one starts on Charlie at once.

"You ought to be ashamed! I don't know why boys like you can't find anything better to do than to go about ruining other people's pleasure."

"Oh, come on, Mona, it's getting worse."

"One can't even admire a lovely view in peace these days. For two pins I'd take you along to the nearest police station and give you in charge for vandalism."

"It's putting me off my tea."

"You've got no sense of decency any of you. Letting off a thing like that in a public place. I don't know what they teach you in schools these days but it certainly isn't

reasonable behaviour. At your age I wouldn't have dared . . ." and so on and so on.

Charlie says nothing. It doesn't seem worth it. Angry ladies never want to have things explained to them anyway. Luckily the smell is being borne away by a brisk sea breeze. At last they hurry away up the prom, the small lady still glaring angrily back at him over her handkerchief.

There's nothing left for Charlie to do but begin the weary trudge home. Rather to his surprise, Ariadne is at the shop door, anxiously looking out for him.

"You O.K., Charlie?"

Charlie tells her the story. He's too tired to make it a good one, but he can't resist adding:

"I caught those boys up, anyway, didn't I? I told you I could run."

"I hope they don't come back," is all Ariadne answers.

2

The next day is bright, with white clouds blowing about the sky like washing escaping from the line. Charlie and Ariadne are sitting on the very end of the pier. Charlie likes to lean right over the rail and watch the sea smashing and crashing against the girders below, but Ariadne doesn't. She tries hard not to look through the cracks between the boards under her feet at the heaving water. The ironwork is all rusty and barnacled and smells of dead fish. It gives her the creeps. Instead she looks back at the Penwyn Bay sea front. The little houses look like toy town, all washed different colours—Auntie Jean's joke shop, the Paradise Fish Saloon, the shop that sells souvenirs and seaside rock, and, at the end of the row, Carlo's Crazy Castle.

This used to be a shop front like all the others, but now it has a false front, painted up to look just like a real castle, with pointed windows and battlements above. A big arched doorway with a portcullis opens on to the pavement. All round it are pictures of kings and queens, skeletons, gypsies, and masked headsmen with axes. Loud notices invite people inside: "SEE INTO THE FUTURE! YOUR FORTUNE TOLD FOR 25p!" "DON'T MISS

CARLO'S WORLD-FAMOUS WAXWORKS! SENSATIONAL AND EDUCATIONAL!" At the side of the entrance is a little glass pay-box, with a smaller notice saying "Closed".

At this moment the trim figure of Mr Carlo Cornetto himself appears at the pay-box window. He turns round the notice so that it reads "Open". Then he steps out in his shirt-sleeves and stands glancing up and down the prom. At one of the castle windows above his head another face appears, that of Mr Cornetto's old dog, Lordy. He sniffs the air with his large black nose, settles down on to his two front paws, and gazes solemnly out to sea. Nobody is about on the prom, only the wheeling, crying gulls. Far up at the other end of the front, beyond the shelters, in a windswept garden of its own, stands the Hydro Hotel. This has a large, grand, red-brick frontage with a great many windows, balconies and turrets, and a long glass veranda running down its entire length. Inside it one or two elderly ladies and gentlemen can be seen sitting in basket chairs, sipping cups of coffee. They, too, gaze out to sea, like castaways scanning the horizon for a friendly sail. Further still, down on the beach, the children of St Ethelred's Holiday Home are playing noisily, digging sandcastles and pouring water all over them-

selves, and one another. The student in charge is crouched in the shelter of a bit of sea-wall, trying to read a newspaper. It is an unequal battle with the wind, which keeps carrying bits of it away. Every few minutes he leaps to his feet to separate squabblers and try to wring the water out of their sopping clothes.

"Not many customers for the shop today," says Ariadne. "Typical, really."

"The coach tours can't park on this side of the bay," says Charlie. "And anyway, they've got really good things over the other side at Penwyn—dodgems and big dippers and fruit machines and all. There's a ghost train too. I wish I had the money to try them. How much money have you got, Ariadne?" he adds hopefully.

"Don't like dodgems much. And I'll bet the ghost train's pathetic," says Ariadne. She doesn't want Charlie to know that she wouldn't dare to go in the ghost train, it's far too scary.

At this moment the joke shop door opens, and Auntie Jean pops out like a cuckoo from a clock, waving them in to lunch. It's fish and chips, Charlie's favourite. This is an extravagance which happens when Auntie Jean forgets to cook anything and has to make a last-minute dash to the Paradise Fish Saloon. They eat in the

crowded back sitting-room, at a wobbly green-topped card table which has a cloth put over it at meal-times. Besides an old sofa and a great many fat armchairs, the room has an old-fashioned coal grate, a treadle sewing-machine on a stand, and a permanent smell of frying. The bold pattern of poppies on the wall-paper is mostly hidden by the various fancy costumes which hang about the room on pegs. These are left over from the time when Auntie Jean worked at the Royalty Theatre. Now it is closed, and the actors and actresses have long since gone away, leaving a good many of their costumes, hats and wigs behind.

"Those boys who stole my stink-bombs have been bothering Mr Cornetto," Auntie Jean tells them as they munch their chips. "He found them trying to get into his place the back way, but old Lordy barked at them, and they ran away. He says they're the two Morgan boys from over at Penwyn. Their Dad runs the Amusement Arcade. No-good boyos, they are. Just let them show their faces here again and I'll give them what for!"

"I don't know what they want to hang about here for," says Ariadne. "They don't need to pinch things from us, when amusement arcades make so much money."

"It's all gambling and razz-me-tazz these days," snorts Auntie Jean. "Penwyn was a very select resort when I first came here—lovely it was. Very high-class hotels, tea dances, band playing every afternoon in the Esplanade Gardens, and shows at the Royalty, of course. Lovely audiences we used to have—packed houses every night."

"Did you act on the stage, Auntie?" asks Charlie.

"Oh no, dear. I was a dresser. Helped the ladies into their clothes, hooked up their corsets, mended their tights, that sort of thing. Mr Cornetto used to go on the stage. He was an acrobat—ever so clever he was."

"I'd like to do that. Or be a conjuror, that'd be even better," says Charlie. "I'd like to put a lady in one of those boxes and pretend to saw her in half."

"Shouldn't think you'd get any lady to let you try," says Ariadne.

At this moment the shop door clangs, and Mr Cornetto himself steps in. He looks downcast. Even his neat black moustache droops at the corners, and his sad brown eyes resemble those of his old spaniel dog, Lordy.

"Cup of tea, Mr Cornetto?" asks Auntie Jean, tea-pot poised.

"Thanks, I won't say no, since you're offering, Mrs

Llanechan Jones. Just closed my place up again for a long dinner-hour, things are that quiet. Hardly worth opening up at all." Mr Cornetto is an Italian, but he sounds Welsh, like Auntie Jean, because he learnt English in Penwyn Bay. "Old Lordy's on guard, looking after things, like. Business has been bad, very bad. My Historical Waxworks, my Hall of Mirrors, people aren't wanting them as they used to. It's all roller-coasters and bingo, see. And now I'm going to have to take down my fortune-telling sign, too. Gypsy Queen Rosita has upped and left me without a word of notice. Gone into business on her own account in Llandudno."

He sups up tea through his moustache and wipes it sadly and carefully on a clean handkerchief.

"*There's* cheeky for you! I could have told you!" cried Auntie Jean. "Gypsy Queen Rosita, indeed! When we all know quite well that she's Mrs Bronwen Evans from the dry-cleaner's in Station Approach! And as for being able to tell the future—why, even old Einstein here could do better." At the sound of his name Einstein, who is lazily extended like a long ginger scarf along the back of the sofa, twitches the tip of his tail and opens one green slit of an eye. "In fact, a great deal better," adds Auntie Jean with respect. "No, don't you mind about *her*, Mr Cornetto. It's good riddance, if you ask me. And with business not being too bright here at the shop either, I'll help you out part-time, like, if I can find my crystal ball."

Auntie Jean is very good at fortune-telling. To prove it, she takes Mr Cornetto's cup and turns it gently in her hands, peering into the tea-leaves at the bottom.

"What does it mean, Auntie?" asks Charlie, leaning over her shoulder.

"Now let me see. You can't get it all at once, you know, Charlie. Looks like a little storm cloud over here, I'm afraid . . . but this is interesting. A person of some importance—a lady, I think."

"Looks more like a poodle-dog to me," says Ariadne.

"No, it's a lady. There's no mistaking her. A relative of yours, perhaps, Mr Cornetto?"

Mr Cornetto is unhelpful.

"No ladies in my family. Not living, that is."

"Perhaps it's a ghost?" suggests Charlie.

"It's a dog. I can see his ears sticking up."

But now Auntie Jean lets out a cry of discovery.

"Well I never, Mr Cornetto! Surely to goodness, I wouldn't have thought it!" she gasps.

"What is it, Auntie?"

"I see a love affair in this cup, as plain as plain. Two hearts as one!"

"Is *that* all?" says Charlie, disappointed.

"And look here! I can see a pound sign! That means money, of course. *There's* lucky for you, as plain as the nose on your face!"

She holds out the cup triumphantly. Mr Cornetto doesn't seem greatly cheered by this news.

"Well, I'll be glad if you'll help me out with the fortune-telling in the afternoons," is all he says. "Clairvoyants being difficult to come by at short notice, so the agency tells me."

They are interrupted by the sound of the shop door being quietly opened. Two figures shuffle in the doorway. It's the Morgan boys again. Slamming down the teacup, Auntie Jean looms out of the back room, hissing with fury. She can be very fierce indeed when she wants to be.

"You leave my stock alone, or I'll have the law on you, and that's only the start!" she spits. "Don't think I don't know your face, Dai Morgan, and yours too, Dylan Morgan, *and* where you live. Get out of this shop before I throw you out myself, and don't come back here or I'll . . ."

But the Morgan boys are gone before she can tell them

what else she's going to do. The others, grouped behind her in the passage, breathe sighs of relief and admiration.

"Thank goodness for that," says Charlie. He doesn't want to have to chase those Morgan boys all over again.

As it happens, the rest of the afternoon turns out quite differently for him.

"Now, I want one of you two to do a little errand for me," says Auntie Jean presently. "There's this box of crackers and paper hats that needs delivering at the Hydro Hotel. The manageress is planning a Carnival entertainment—trying to cheer the place up, see. Though how she's going to manage it with that lot that's staying up there, I don't know."

"I've got to write a postcard home," says Ariadne quickly, eyeing her book.

As there seems to be nobody else to offer, it's decided that Charlie shall go. The box he has to deliver is a large one, not very heavy, but bulky enough. Charlie sets off up the narrow streets behind the prom, carrying it first under one arm, then under the other, and ends by balancing it on his head with his cap turned back to front. Like this he climbs up the imposing front drive of the Hydro Hotel, marches up the front steps, and enters the

large hall, blinking in the dimness. It is completely
empty. There is a big counter of polished wood with a
vase of flowers on it, and a notice saying "Reception.
Please ring." Charlie dumps down his box, adjusts his
cap, and rings. Nobody comes. He rings again, loudly.
Still nobody. While he waits, Charlie begins to wander
about, admiring the little pink lamps on the round tables
and trying out the huge padded armchairs. Far away in
the hotel he can hear voices and the faint noise of vacu-
uming. He comes to a wide staircase, sweeping down
into the hall and dividing into two flights at the bottom.
This might be so that two people could race each other
and see who reaches the hall first, thinks Charlie. In the
middle is a huge, old-fashioned lift shaft, like a great iron
cage with a glass box inside it. The lift doors stand open.

Charlie steps inside and presses the button marked
"Basement". Immediately the doors close, the lift gives
way pleasurably under him, purrs downwards, and stops.
At once Charlie presses another button marked "4th
Floor". The lift glides upwards. He has been in plenty of
lifts before, of course, but in this one you can see the
staircase moving past through the glass. He presses
another button—fifth floor this time—then down again
to the ground floor.

"Five, four, three, two, one—we have lift-off," mutters Charlie, and up he goes again to the fourth floor, changes his mind, presses the third floor button in midflight. Then he starts to go up and down like a yo-yo, pressing all the buttons at random, and watching the bannisters slide giddily by. He is at the very top of the building, and dropping down to the basement again for the sixth time, when the lift suddenly gives a jolt, a shudder, and stops abruptly between floors. Charlie presses all the buttons, one at a time. Nothing happens. He tries again. Still the lift doesn't move. He struggles to open the doors, but they remain firmly shut.

"I'm stuck," says Charlie to himself.

And then, aloud, with panic rising, "Oh, help, I'm stuck!"

3

Downstairs in the hotel lounge Mrs Cadwallader and her sister-in-law, Miss Mona Cadwallader, are taking afternoon tea. They sit surrounded by a dense jungle of palms, looking out at the windy sea. Inside the temperature is tropical. The guests at the Hydro have to be kept very warm, like tomatoes under glass. Miss Mona perches upright on the edge of her chair. She resembles a neat bird of prey, now and again dipping daintily into her teacup. Mrs Cadwallader, a large lady with blonde curls arranged like an enormous pile of bubbles on top of her head, lies back among the cushions. A great many necklaces and rings sparkle gaily about her, but her mouth droops.

"Boring," she says. "A really boring view I call this—all those waves. Makes me seasick. They're not even blue! And it's not as though there's many people on the beach either. If we were in the Bahamas, now, that'd be a different matter."

"It's time for our walk, Connie, dear," murmurs Miss Mona, carefully ignoring these remarks, all of which she has heard before. "Which shall it be? A stroll on the pier, or up to the headland?"

"I'm sick to death of the headland," answers Mrs Cadwallader crossly. "We go there every afternoon when we don't go on the pier, and either way we get blown to bits. I'm sick of the prom, too. Nothing happening there, either, except nasty little boys dropping stink-bombs all over the place. It isn't as if there were any good slot-machines. Why don't we go over to Penwyn this afternoon and give the Fun Fair a try? Might see a bit of life over there at least. We could find out what's on at the cinema."

Miss Mona raises her eyebrows. She has two pairs. The real ones are plucked and the others are thinly pencilled in half an inch higher up.

"I can't think why you're always wanting to go over to that vulgar place, Connie. It's completely tasteless and without any kind of attraction, as far as I can see. We did come here for a quiet holiday for old times' sake, after all."

"Quiet all right! More like a graveyard. Penwyn isn't a bit like I remember it years ago. Anyway, I keep telling you I don't need a rest. I'm just bored stiff."

Miss Mona smiles patiently and consults her tiny watch.

"If you don't want to join me in a walk, dear, I think

I'll just pop out for a little blow on my own. I'll see you upstairs half an hour before dinner. Don't forget to allow plenty of time to change, will you? You know the manageress likes us to be punctual."

"Punctual, indeed!" snorts Mrs Cadwallader. "Nothing worth being punctual *for*!"

She remains in her chair, staring gloomily out of the window. Presently she sees Miss Mona in a headscarf, setting briskly out along the prom. Mrs Cadwallader rises and looks about the lounge for someone else to talk to, but there is nobody left except old Colonel Quickly, snoozing underneath his newspaper. Sighing, she wanders into the hall and rings for the lift.

As she waits for it to arrive, she is already wishing that she hadn't spoken so crossly to her sister-in-law. Mona's patience is often a reproach to her. They have lived together in hotels ever since Mrs Cadwallader's husband died, and have had many such conversations. Mrs Cadwallader is very rich, because her husband left her all his money, and the family jewellery. Miss Mona, on the other hand, is not well off at all. So she accompanies Mrs Cadwallader from one hotel to another trying to get her to behave properly, in a genteel manner. She has very little success. Mrs Cadwallader doesn't care what people

think of her, and misses her old knock-about life terribly. She was on the stage before she married her husband, Caddy, who was a devil-may-care fellow, who liked driving about in a fast open car and played tennis in sparkling white trousers. How unlike his sister, Mona, he was. And how Mona had disapproved of the way they both whirled about the world, going to parties, cinemas and motor-racing, and doing nothing but enjoy themselves.

Mrs Cadwallader sighs again, thinking of those happy, long-lost days.

"Boring, that's what it is," she says, and rings for the lift again. Nothing happens. She is very put out. Her room is on the fourth floor, and she hates walking upstairs. What is more, this is the third time the lift has failed to arrive since she has been staying at this hotel. She looks about for somebody to complain to, but there is nobody. Frowning, she sets off up the stairs. She has reached the half-landing between the second and third floors when she hears a knocking noise. She stops and looks up the stairwell. She can see the bottom half of the lift with a pair of legs inside it. It is from here that the noise comes. Walking up a few more stairs, she peers in through the thick plate glass. Charlie Moon's face looks back at her like a goldfish from a bowl.

"I'm stuck," he says. But Mrs Cadwallader can only see his lips move silently, making him look even more like a goldfish than before.

"What are you doing in there?" she asks severely.

"I'M STUCK!" shouts Charlie. He is red in the face with anger and fright. He bangs on the lift door, points up, points down, rattles the door as hard as he can.

"Aaaaah, I *see*! You're *stuck*," says Mrs Cadwallader more kindly. She doesn't recognize Charlie as the boy on the prom, under the big peak of his cap. "Well, you're not the first one. That lift is a danger to the public. A disgrace, that's what it is."

She signals to him to stay where he is, and goes off to get help. Charlie hasn't really any other alternative, so he settles down to wait as patiently as he can. After a while, back comes Mrs Cadwallader with the hotel handyman. He in turn goes off to fetch a ladder, grumbling in Welsh, and disappears up into the roof to wrestle with the ancient machinery that works the lift. Mrs Cadwallader remains, now joined by one or two other guests, smiling encouragingly at Charlie and making cheery remarks. She has quite forgotten her bad mood in all the excitement. To Charlie the time seems endless. He wonders if he will ever get out of this horrible glass

(33)

box, but he feels too exposed to give way to despair. Instead he pulls the peak of his red-and-white cap down over his eyes and huddles in a corner, ignoring everyone.

At last the lift gives a violent jerk. Then it moves shakily down to the second floor landing, and the doors open. Charlie is free at last! By this time a small crowd has gathered, including the manageress herself, who is extremely cross. Everyone wants to know what Charlie has been up to, getting himself stuck in the lift like that and causing so much trouble. Eyeing the stairs and longing to get away, he starts wearily to explain about the box of Carnival novelties, which he hopes is still sitting in the hall. But at this moment Mrs Cadwallader steps forward and, much to his embarrassment, throws an arm protectively round his shoulders.

"Don't keep asking him questions. Can't you see he's all upset, poor little chap? Quite green round the gills, he is. You'll be lucky if his Mum doesn't prosecute. I know I would if I was her, an' all!" And with this, she steps smartly back into the lift, pulling Charlie with her, presses the button marked "Basement" and they both disappear instantly from view.

The basement floor of the Hydro Hotel is almost entirely

occupied by the ballroom. These days it remains nearly always empty, save for a lot of dust and rows and rows of tiny gold chairs, ranged about the walls like ladies waiting for a dance. At one end of it, in a place where an orchestra used to sit, is a glossy black piano. Charlie and Mrs Cadwallader step out into an echoing half-light, with a faint lingering smell of face-powder, stale tobacco smoke and linoleum. Then Mrs Cadwallader finds a switch and the room is filled at once with a piercing rose-coloured glow.

Charlie is very relieved to have been rescued from the lift, and from trying to explain what he was doing in there in the first place, but he is not at all pleased to find himself alone in a ballroom with Mrs Cadwallader. He is hot, confused and exhausted, and he wants to go home. What's more he is troubled by the uncomfortable feeling that at any moment he may be recognized. So far it's clear that he hasn't been, but under these lights it's a bit risky. This could mean more trouble.

"Thank you very much. I think I'd better be getting back now," says Charlie. "My Auntie's expecting me."

But Mrs Cadwallader pays no attention to this. She lights a cigarette in a long green holder.

"Terrible hotel, this," she tells him, "what with that

lift breaking down, and the hot-water pipes juddering and gurgling in my bedroom at some ungodly hour in the morning, and the food stone-cold half the time. I'd walk out tomorrow if I thought I could get in anywhere else."

"It's just that my Auntie . . ."

"When things aren't going wrong or breaking down, it's like a graveyard. All those old fogies. I like a bit of life myself. Music, dancing, that sort of thing." She puffs out cigarette smoke in the direction of the piano. "I was in the theatre, you see."

"Yes, so was my Auntie. But . . ."

"Very slim I was in those days. You live round here, dear?"

"I'm staying at my Auntie's. As a matter of fact she's expecting . . ."

"On holiday, are you?"

Charlie nods.

"So are we, me and my sister-in-law. I like the big resorts, but she likes it very quiet, very refined. When we were in Spain last year Mona was the one who complained. Too noisy and too hot, she said, and the food gave her a liver attack. Talk about a moaner! She never stopped! Didn't like the guests in the hotel—said they weren't the right type—didn't like the dancing." She

glances at the empty ballroom. "I love a dance myself. I wonder when they last had one here?"

Before Charlie can answer Mrs Cadwallader sets off across the huge shiny floor, humming a tune, and holding her cigarette holder out at arm's length with her other arm about the shoulders of an imaginary partner. Her high-heeled shoes swerve in all directions making a complicated pattern of steps.

"I think I ought to be . . ." calls out Charlie after her, but she doesn't seem to hear. She reaches the piano. Sitting down, she balances her cigarette-holder on the end of the key-board, removes her rings, and strikes up a thrilling chord. Then she bursts into song.

"WALTZ-ing WALTZ-ing, HIGH in the clouds.

ON-ly YOU and I in the clouds . . ."

carols Mrs Cadwallader sweetly.

Charlie sits down on one of the little gold chairs, defeated. She sings on and on, playing more runs and trills on the piano than anyone could have believed possible. Between verses she beams over at him, for all the world as though he were a proper audience. Charlie begins to feel desperate. At last delivery comes. The lift doors at the other end of the room open, and out steps Miss Mona. Mrs Cadwallader's song falters

in mid-flow, and her hands drop from the key-board.

"So here you are, Connie," says Miss Mona quietly. "I hope you realize what time it is? Dinner is in ten minutes." She looks coldly at Charlie. "Is this the boy who got stuck in the lift? I heard all about it from the manageress herself, when I came in from my walk. She was really annoyed. We've been looking all over the hotel for both of you. What on earth have you been doing in here, anyway?"

"Just having a bit of fun," says Mrs Cadwallader defiantly, but she shuts up the piano lid all the same. "I was just giving this little lad a song or two."

Miss Mona fixes Charlie with a beady eye.

"I feel I've seen you before," she says. "What is your name?"

"Charlie Moon," answers Charlie, pulling down his cap even further over his eyes.

"Where do you live?"

"I'm staying with my Auntie who runs the Joke and Carnival Novelty shop along opposite the pier, and I think if you don't mind she'll be expecting . . ."

"*I* know who you are!" snaps Miss Mona, looking at him more closely under the peak. "You're the little vandal who was behaving so disgustingly on the prom

yesterday. You're an obvious trouble-maker, that's clear. I suppose you thought you could come trespassing in this hotel and making more mischief without being recognized? Now, listen to me. You're to leave here at once and if I hear of your causing any more trouble I'm going straight to the police."

"Oh, come on, Mona," says Mrs Cadwallader. "He wasn't doing anything."

"*Straight* to the police, do you understand? Now come along, Connie, we must change. We're terribly late already."

Taking Mrs Cadwallader's arm, Miss Mona sweeps her into the lift. As the doors close, Mrs Cadwallader catches Charlie's eye over the top of her sister-in-law's head, and gives him a big wink.

Left alone at last, Charlie breathes a great sigh of relief. It has been a long, difficult afternoon. He is sick to death of the Hydro Hotel and everyone in it. He never wants to see any of them again. But, as he turns to go, something catches his eye, twinkling on top of the grand piano. Drawing nearer, he sees three rings lying there—very expensive-looking rings with stones nearly as big as boiled sweets. Mrs Cadwallader has left them behind!

"You still here, then?" says the hotel handyman sternly. Charlie has collided with him as he tears upstairs with the three rings in his pocket. "You'd better not let the manageress catch you. She's in a black, bad temper, indeed. And, look you, don't go messing about with that lift again, or I'll have you for sure. I've got enough to do here without young tomfool boyos like yourself tinkering about all over the place."

"Those two ladies," pants Charlie, "they've just gone upstairs. I've got to catch them!"

"If it's the Cadwallader ladies you mean, they've gone to their rooms, no doubt, as it's nearly time for dinner. What do you want them for, anyway?"

"There's something I've got to give them. It's important."

"Well, right-ho then. But you're to come straight down again, mind. They're on the fourth floor. I can't recall the big lady's room number off the top of me head, but the other one's in Number 404."

"Thanks!" shouts Charlie over his shoulder. He's already sprinting up the next flight of stairs, two at a time. No more lift journeys for him.

The Hydro seems to have as many rooms, passages and stairs in it as an enchanted palace in a fairy tale, and

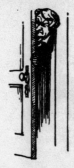

to be just as confusing. Reaching the fourth floor, Charlie takes off from the main staircase, scurrying like the White Rabbit down long corridors, and counting the room numbers backwards under his breath as he passes. Nobody is about. Most of the guests are already gathered for dinner downstairs. Through open doors he glimpses marble bathrooms, dignified mahogany beds with starched white sheets, and the occasional small, startled reflection of himself in a huge wardrobe mirror. At last he arrives at room Number 404 and knocks timidly.

Miss Mona's questing, bird-like face appears almost immediately.

"Is this intended to be some sort of joke?" she says angrily, before Charlie can get in a word. "You have no business to be up here, as you well know. I won't tell you again. Kindly leave these premises *at once*, or I'll call the manageress."

"I . . . the other lady . . ."

"You mean my sister-in-law? She's dressing for dinner. What do you want with her?"

"I found . . . I mean, she left these behind on the piano!"

Charlie plunges his hand into his pocket and pulls out

the three rings. They lie winking and sparkling on his palm. Miss Mona looks at them silently for a moment.

"I see," she says, in a slightly altered tone. "That was most careless. I will see that they are returned at once."

She takes the rings into her own hand and half closes the door. Then she adds, through the crack:

"Thank you for returning them promptly. Now please LEAVE HERE AT ONCE!"

The door is then closed firmly in Charlie's face, and he is left standing alone in the corridor. Tired as he is, he breaks into a wild, capering dance, throwing his cap about, thumbing his nose, and pulling hideous faces at the closed door. Then, turning away, he starts to try and find his way back to the main staircase. At last he can go home for his tea.

4

"Lovely bit of material, that is," says Auntie Jean, holding up a gentleman's tailcoat, one of the many items of costume that she keeps in her back sitting-room. "Bit of moth under the arm here, but good as new otherwise."

She blows the dust off the shoulders of the coat, and it rises in a great cloud.

"What's that purple dress, Auntie, with the black lace on it?" asks Ariadne. She and Charlie are sitting side by side on the sofa, eating sticky buns.

"Oooooh, that's a dream, that is. It's an old-fashioned costume, once worn by the leading lady in a musical play at the Royalty. A real picture she was in it, too."

"It's just like the sort of dress the ladies in my book are wearing. I'd love to sweep about with that train thing behind."

"What's that shaggy brown one over there?" Charlie wants to know.

"Some sort of animal suit, I think, Charlie. It was for the pantomime one year, if I remember right. Looks as though it needs a bit of a patch in it when I get a moment. Lovely on, though."

Auntie Jean is in good spirits. She loves going through

the old costumes and reminding herself of happy times in the theatre. It is the day after Charlie's adventure in the lift, and it has been a successful one in the shop. A party of trippers strayed in during a shower and all bought false noses to cheer themselves up on the way home.

"I've got some lovely pork chops for tea," she tells them. "And chocolate ice-cream to follow—a treat, see. Why don't you slip along and ask Mr Cornetto if he wants to come round and join us? He looks as though he could do with a good meal. I don't believe he cooks anything proper, there on his own."

Charlie and Ariadne stroll up the prom, still chewing the remains of their buns. The sun has come out, warming the damp pavement under their feet, and catching the sails of two little boats, dipping along optimistically in the bay. The tide has gone out, leaving behind it a glittering expanse of rich, salty mud, garlanded with dark seaweed. In the middle distance, the children from St Ethelred's Holiday Home are straggling along the water-line, with melted ice-lollies dribbling down to their elbows. They stop now again to poke about amongst the driftwood, or push one another into the pools. The student in charge, his trousers rolled up to the knee, moves up and down his flock like a sheep-dog,

herding them home to bed. Their voices echo across the bay as in an enormous bathroom.

Charlie and Ariadne arrive at Carlo's Crazy Castle to find Lordy in charge of the pay-box, his fore-paws on the till. He greets them with loud barks, which bring Mr Cornetto hurrying to the entrance. He winds up the portcullis to let them in.

"Well, there's kind of you, I'm sure!" he exclaims, when they deliver Auntie Jean's invitation. "I'm just closing up here. I'd a few people round earlier, but it's pretty quiet on the whole. Want to see round for free, while you're here, do you?"

He leads the way into an entrance hall, strangely decorated in a style half way between a medieval castle and a tea-bar. There are suits of armour, a life-sized bear carved out of wood, some plastic-topped tables and chairs, and rows of old-fashioned slot-machines ranged about the walls. There is also a gilt mirror or two, some shields and helmets, and a piano with pictures of storks and flowers painted upon it. At one end of the room is an archway, covered with a heavy velvet curtain, marked "HALL OF WAXWORKS". Another archway at the other end has a curtain of beads with a notice saying "GYPSY QUEEN ROSITA. FORTUNE-TELLER AND CLAIRVOYANT".

But over this is pasted another notice with the words "Temporarily Closed".

Mr Cornetto ushers them proudly into the Hall of Waxworks. Two rows of shabby lurching figures are arranged along low platforms, behind looped silk cords. Ariadne, who is fond of History, knows who most of them are without having to read the labels—Napoleon, Queen Elizabeth the First, Sir Francis Drake, Nelson, Christopher Columbus. There are other, more sinister characters, too—Dick Turpin, the highwayman, with a cocked hat and levelled pistols, and, at the far end of the room, a tableau of Mary Queen of Scots with a masked Executioner, who looks as though he is getting ready to chop off her head.

"That one's great," says Charlie. "He's really scary!"

"I like her dress—all those pearls," agrees Ariadne.

The waxworks return their gaze with glassy eyes.

"And now, the Hall of Mirrors," says Mr Cornetto, throwing open another door. They pass through it into a maze of their own reflections. In one mirror Charlie is as round and fat as Humpty Dumpty. In the next he is as tall and thin as if he had been pulled out like chewing-gum, and his eyes seem to meet in the middle of his head.

Standing together, a little further on, he and Ariadne appear as two giants, their feet miles away, their bodies ballooning out round the middle, and their giggling faces flattened out like saucers.

"Bet you look like that when you're grown up," says Charlie. "You could get a job on the telly as one of those monsters from outer space."

But Ariadne doesn't bother to answer back. She has already moved on to see, reflected over and over again, an endless vista of herself, in which every small movement turns her into a forest of arms or an army of legs.

"Like being a centipede," she murmurs. "But where do I—or rather, where does *it*—end?"

But Mr Cornetto is already leading the way through the mirror maze into another smaller room with more slot-machines in it and a huge weighing-machine which says "I SPEAK YOUR WEIGHT", past a small door marked "Private", which leads upstairs to the little flat where he and Lordy have their living arrangements, then back to the entrance hall.

"Now, I've just got to lock up and give Lordy his supper," says Mr Cornetto, when they have admired everything. "I won't be long. You two go ahead and tell your Auntie I'll be along about a quarter to seven, if that

suits. Lordy can stay here and look after things while I'm out."

The evening sunlight on the airy prom seems very reassuring after the dusty fantasies of Carlo's Crazy Castle.

"Those slot-machines are a bit . pathetic," says Ariadne on the way back, "sort of old-fashioned. I've seen *much* better ones in the Amusement Arcade over at Penwyn. They have lots of flashing lights and things, and you can win a whole pile of money on them—well, sometimes you can. I liked the Hall of Mirrors, though."

"And the waxworks," Charlie adds, "specially that one with Queen Elizabeth having her head chopped off."

"Mary Queen of Scots, Charlie. Don't you know *any* History?"

"Course I do. But we haven't done that bit. At our school it's all projects—Roman walls and roads and that. Not many battles. We did some good stuff once about the Barbarian Hordes sweeping across Europe, but then we had a new teacher and went back to roads again. Do you think Mr Cornetto gets many customers?"

"Doesn't seem like it. As bad as Auntie Jean's—absolutely typically pathetic, in fact," says Ariadne, greatly

cheered, as always, by being able to use both her favourite words at once.

The shop door is already closed, with the blind pulled down, so they go round the back, to be met by the delicious smell of frying pork chops and onions. Auntie Jean is in her little kitchen, darting about in a cloud of smoke and steam, with Einstein weaving excitedly round her legs. Hungry as hunters, Charlie and Ariadne start to lay the table in the sitting-room, putting on a clean checked table-cloth. There is a loud, insistent knocking at the shop door.

"That'll be Mr Cornetto, I expect," calls out Auntie Jean. "He's early. Just let him in, will you, Charlie, dear?"

But the shadow Charlie sees on the blind at the end of the passage is far too big to be Mr Cornetto's. When he unlocks the door and opens it there, as large as life, is Mrs Cadwallader, beaming and looking very grand in pink and pearls. She sweeps right past him into the shop.

"I'm *so* glad I got your address right, dear," she says. "I felt I just had to thank you personally for returning both my rings to me yesterday. It really was silly of me to leave them lying about like that. Mona was furious, of

course. I'm always doing it, you see. The things I've lost! You wouldn't believe it! Valuable, too. The trouble is, I can never remember what I've put on in the morning when I take it off at night. And then, of course, when I find I've lost something, it's too late to look for it. Little Scatterbrain, my poor late husband used to call me. But you saved me this time, and no mistake. I wanted to give you this, as a little token of my appreciation."

She presses a pound into Charlie's hand, and airily waves away his thanks.

"So this is your Auntie's shop," she continues, looking about her at the masks and false noses. "I like a joke myself—always have done. Poor Mona's got no sense of humour, I'm afraid, and that's a fact. Only the other day . . . Good heavens above!" Her flow of chatter stops abruptly, as though she has seen a ghost. Over the top of Charlie's head she has caught sight of Auntie Jean, standing in the doorway in her big flowered apron.

"I don't believe it!" gasps Mrs Cadwallader, clutching her pearls.

"It can't be . . . !" cries Auntie Jean.

"Well, I never did!"

"Connie!"

"Jean Jones!"

"Indeed to goodness me, where on earth did you spring from after all these years?"

Charlie, open-mouthed, just manages to step neatly out of the way as the two ladies come together in the middle of the shop in a hearty embrace.

"Come right inside, Connie, dear," says Auntie Jean, ushering Mrs Cadwallader through into the back room and sitting her down in the best armchair. "You children, lay another place at the table. We've another guest for tea!"

As the two ladies fall to chattering and laughing and exclaiming both at once, like a pair of noisy parakeets, Charlie and Ariadne, goggling with astonishment, try to piece together the explanation for this surprising reunion. Bit by bit, they find out that Mrs Cadwallader, in her days on the stage, once played a summer season at the Royalty Theatre. Auntie Jean was working there then as a dresser, and the two became firm friends. But after Mrs Cadwallader married her rich husband they somehow drifted apart, and haven't laid eyes on one another again until this very moment.

"Well, fancy your being the lady that saved this young scamp nephew of mine from being stuck in the lift yesterday," says Auntie Jean. "What a small world it is,

indeed! And you one of those posh folk staying up at the Hydro!"

"I'm staying there with my sister-in-law, Mona. But they're an unfriendly lot up there. Nobody talks to anybody. Things aren't a bit like they used to be. Even the old Royalty's closed, I see."

"Yes, sad isn't it? The dear old Royalty. The times we had there, Connie! All that rush and excitement before the curtain went up, and you such a picture in those white tights and all those sparkling sequins!"

"Oh, it's such years ago now. But seeing you here makes it seem like yesterday," says Mrs Cadwallader happily. "Do you remember, Jean, that roll of drums from the orchestra pit, then *smash* went the cymbals, and up I went into the air, as light as a feather!"

"And I was always that frightened in case you fell off! There you were on that pyramid of strong men, all standing on top of one another's shoulders, with you at the very top! I never knew how you had the nerve, Connie, really I don't!"

"Oh, that was nothing to me in those days. I was a dancer, as you know, before I joined that troupe of acrobats. And I could sing too, of course. In fact, I was

running through a few old numbers with your nephew here. Quite carried away I was. But I'm a bit out of practice for acrobatics, I'm afraid—put on a little bit of weight recently."

"You remember Mr Cornetto of course?"

"Carlo Cornetto? Why, of course. He was one of the troupe, you know. Lovely acrobat, he was, but couldn't speak a word of English, as I remember. Just used to smile and show his white teeth."

"He's retired now and settled down right here in Penwyn Bay. Took a fancy to the place, learnt to speak English lovely, and now he's running the Crazy Castle down at the far end of the prom. I'm expecting him here at any moment, as a matter of fact. Oh my goodness, those pork chops will be burned if I don't have a look at them. Is that him now? Quick, children, run and let him in!"

Mr Cornetto has changed into his best suit and is wearing a silk bow tie that resembles a large yellow spotted butterfly. He is so surprised to see Mrs Cadwallader that for the moment he forgets all his English and bursts into a flow of excited Italian, clasping both her hands and kissing them over and over again. At last Auntie Jean manages to sit everyone down at the table. Mr Cornetto soon regains his command of English, and

throughout the meal all three grown-ups talk and talk, reminding one another of past dramas and excitements behind the scenes at the Royalty, of old friends long since forgotten, and telling one another over and over again how little they have changed, and how they would have known each other anywhere. Charlie and Ariadne attack their food in silence, and escape as soon as possible into the kitchen to finish up the remains of the chocolate ice-cream in peace.

"I'm getting a bit sick of the old Royalty," says Ariadne, licking her spoon thoroughly. "They don't half go on about it—that Mrs Cadwallader especially. Can't she talk!"

"Wait till she starts singing," answers Charlie.

"I don't see how anybody could have lifted her up into the air, not even a whole troupe of acrobats. You'd need a *crane*, if you ask me."

"She's given me a quid, though."

"Oooooh, lucky! What for?"

"Getting her rings back for her. It's funny, though . . ."

"What's funny?"

"When she thanked me just now, she said for both her rings."

"Well?"

"But there were three of them, all whoppers. I remember them quite well because I had them in my pocket."

"I expect she made a mistake."

"She's only got two of them on now. I looked when Mr Cornetto was carrying on, using all those foreign words and kissing her hands."

"Perhaps she's left the other one somewhere else by now. She seems pretty dotty, if you ask me."

At this moment they both become aware of a lull in the flow of chatter coming from the sitting-room. They stop licking their spoons and look towards the door. Einstein, who has been finishing up the remains of the pork chops under the sink, also looks up, his ears cocked. Then the lull gives way to another much more piercing sound. Einstein, with bristling fur, bolts like lightning through the pantry window. Mrs Cadwallader has started to sing.

5

It's Thursday afternoon—early closing day at the Joke and Carnival Novelty Shop—and all is confusion in the little back room. Auntie Jean, wearing a gypsy costume and shawl, with a bright scarf tied over her hair and a great many jangling bracelets and beads, is pulling everything about in a frantic search for her crystal ball. She is expected at the Crazy Castle to tell fortunes at two o'clock sharp. In the passage the piled-up boxes are spilling out their contents all over the floor—packets of paper streamers, gigantic false teeth and plates of plastic fried eggs are everywhere, but no crystal ball. Charlie, who started by trying to help, has found a camera which shoots out a rubber snake when you press the button, and he is trying it out on Einstein, who sits solidly on the dresser, his eyes half closed in disgust. In the midst of it all, Ariadne is curled up in an armchair, reading.

"Come out of that book, Ariadne, do, and give us a hand," cries Auntie Jean in anguish. "If I can't find the dratted thing I won't get any fortunes told today!"

Ariadne drags her eyes unwillingly from the page. Balancing herself with one hand on her book, to keep

her place, she hangs upside down over the seat and peers under the sagging frill.

"There's something under here, I think. Oooooh, what a lot of fluff!" She gropes about and pulls out a long pink silk scarf and a green cigarette case, along with a cloud of dust.

"Now whatever have you got there?" says Auntie Jean, bending down to inspect them closely.

"Not your crystal ball, I'm afraid. Perhaps they belong to Mrs Cadwallader. I think this scarf matches the dress she was wearing when she came the other evening."

"I believe you're right! That's her cigarette case for sure."

"She must be awfully absent-minded, leaving her things behind all the time, I mean. First the rings that Charlie found, and now these. Typical, I suppose."

"You'd better slip up to the Hydro and give them back to her. Pop them into a package with her name on it, so you only have to leave them at the reception desk."

"Oh, all right," says Ariadne, "I'll do it when I've finished this chapter."

Auntie Jean resumes her search, with a great deal more commotion and fuss. At last the crystal ball is discovered under a bit of blanket in Einstein's cat

basket. It has to be well washed and polished before being restored to its black velvet coverings. Ten minutes late already, Auntie Jean whisks her shawl straight and bustles away up the prom.

"Walk up to the Hydro with us, Charlie," asks Ariadne, throwing down her book and yawning.

"No thanks, not likely," says Charlie. "I'm not going up there again. I hate the place. And anyway the Old Moaner might catch me."

"How pathetic," says Ariadne. "Oh well, I suppose I'll have to go on my own."

Having put Mrs Cadwallader's things into a package and addressed it carefully in large curly letters with her felt pen, Ariadne strolls off with it under her arm, up the hill to the Hydro. Today the reception desk in the big hall is attended by the manageress herself, who is busy with a typewriter and a great deal of paper work. She hardly raises her eyes as Ariadne enters.

"I suppose you've come about the job," she says. "It's only the one time, you know. We need extra help because of the Carnival Lunch we're having, but otherwise we're perfectly well suited. How old are you?"

"Thirteen," says Ariadne promptly. She is really only twelve, but can never resist adding on a year.

The manageress looks her up and down over her glasses.

"Well, I really had someone older in mind. I'm not allowed to employ anyone of your age on a permanent basis, of course. You look like a reliable girl, though. It's just to help the waitress and clear up afterwards. Can you lay tables?"

"Yes, I can."

"Well, you might do. I'll take your name and address at any rate."

"I'm Mrs Jean Jones' niece, from the joke shop on the prom, but I haven't come after the job," Ariadne manages to tell her. "I've brought this. One of the ladies staying in this hotel, Mrs Cadwallader, left some things behind when she came to see us the other evening." And she puts the package down on the desk.

"Oh, I see. Why didn't you say so before? Mrs Cadwallader and her sister-in-law are in the Palm Lounge at this moment, I believe, so you can give them to her now if you like. It's just over there, to the left."

Ariadne shuffles her feet and stays where she is.

"Well?" asks the manageress. She has already turned her eyes back to her papers.

"I'd like to take the job if you want someone. I could

help the waitress like you said. And I can wash up, too."

The manageress looks at her again. After a bit she says:

"Well, as I know your aunt I'll give you a try. But only if she gives her permission first, mind. We'll pay you 75p an hour and you get a free meal. I'll need you here on Saturday week at twelve noon, sharp. Don't forget now."

"I'll be here," says Ariadne. Inwardly she is surprised at herself for making such a sudden decision. As she writes her name and address, she is already wondering what Auntie Jean will say, and if she will allow her to work at the Hydro. She hadn't really meant to ask for the job, or to pretend to be older than she is. Somehow the words just slipped out. But the manageress has already returned to her work, and the matter seems to be settled. Picking up the package, Ariadne goes off in the direction of the Palm Lounge.

At first she can't see Mrs Cadwallader anywhere. The huge room is nearly empty. Walking all round it, she soon hears low, angry voices coming from a little alcove, hidden by a forest of foliage.

". . . vulgar in the extreme," hisses one voice, and Mrs Cadwallader answers:

"You're always trying to spoil my fun, Mona. Just because I meet up with a couple of old friends and have a chat about old times, you have to try and stop me."

"I just don't think they're suitable people for you to mix with," says Miss Mona. "That awful joke shop. I've never seen so much cheap rubbish in all my life. And who is this Italian with his ridiculous side-show?"

"It's not ridiculous. He'd be doing very good business if he were over at Penwyn. Just needs a bit of brightening up, that's all. He was a lovely acrobat, too, in the old days, when I first knew him. He could do four back somersaults and land on his hands, no trouble at all, and then jump up into the air like a jack-rabbit! You should have seen him!"

"I'm very glad I didn't. I should have thought you'd want to forget about your previous career, now you have a social position to keep up."

"It was *me* that Caddy married, after all," retorts Mrs Cadwallader, "and *he* didn't give tuppence for social position!"

Before Miss Mona can answer this, Ariadne clears her throat loudly and edges round the potted palms, with the package held out before her.

"Well, I never did!" says Mrs Cadwallader, after greeting her warmly. "What's this? Don't tell me I left

these behind at your Auntie's? I've been looking for them everywhere."

Miss Mona eyes Ariadne with annoyance.

"Really, Connie," is all she says. "Isn't that the cigarette case you had as a wedding present? I wish you'd try to look after your things better. Give those to me right away. I'll take them upstairs for you."

Mrs Cadwallader ignores her.

"You're a good lass," she tells Ariadne. "A pair of good kids, you and your cousin. I'm grateful to you both. Here's a pound. And as you're here, I'll walk back with you to your Auntie's for a breath of air."

"She's telling fortunes at Mr Cornetto's this afternoon," Ariadne tells her. "She's ever so good at it. But I don't need a reward, really."

"Take it, dear. Never refuse money when it's honestly earned. So Jean's fortune-telling at the Crazy Castle, is she? I think I'll go along there, then, and see how she's getting on." She rises to her feet, and winds the long pink scarf several times round her neck with a flourish. "Cheerio, Mona. See you later, alligator, as we say in Show Business!"

Miss Mona does not answer, but the tilt of her small beak of a nose makes her feelings very plain.

6

"More life! More sparkle! Music, lights, razzle-dazzle!" exclaims Mrs Cadwallader, waving her scarf about.

"What was that last one again?" asks Mr Cornetto cautiously.

"Razzle-dazzle. Excitement, glitter—*you* know. It's what this place needs."

"Oh, yes. I see." Mr Cornetto chews his moustache thoughtfully.

The Crazy Castle has closed for the day, and they are all eating ham sandwiches at one of the little round tables in the entrance hall. Auntie Jean is still wearing her gypsy costume. There have been more visitors than usual that afternoon, and she has seen a good many exciting futures in her crystal ball.

"Apart from a lick of paint and a good smarten up, you need some kind of special attraction," continues Mrs Cadwallader. "Something that'll bring in the crowds—as well as Jean's fortune-telling, of course."

"What about lots of gambling-machines?" says Ariadne. "Or a space-machine like they've got over at Penwyn?"

Mr Cornetto shakes his head.

"Things like that cost a lot of money, and I've hardly any in the bank. The bank manager keeps writing me letters about it."

"When Mum and I went to the circus," says Charlie, "there were people outside the big tent, dressed up, beating a drum and shouting 'Roll up! Roll up!' to get people to come inside."

"My word, that's given me an idea, Charlie!" cries Mrs Cadwallader excitedly. "You know those old costumes you've got at your place, Jean? We could have an Old Time Night here—you know, dressed in old-fashioned costumes, and getting people to join in with songs that they all remember. I could lead the singing—and you can still play the piano, can't you, Carlo?"

"Oh yes, indeed. But I'm not sure . . ."

"We could open up the portcullis here and have coloured lights. And we could smarten up the waxworks, too, while we're at it. Re-hang the curtains, polish up the mirrors, all that kind of thing. I'll help with the expenses."

"And I'll help with the sewing if I can," says Auntie Jean. "Come on, now, Mr Cornetto. Things are that slack at the joke shop this season, I'll have to close down if we can't attract some more people over here some-

how. Anything's worth a try. Would you children be kind enough to help out, d'you think?"

"I could paint up some of the pictures of kings and queens and things on the front of the building," offers Ariadne. "I'm good at painting. I hardly ever go over the lines."

"I'll polish up the magic mirrors, if you like," says Charlie.

"You're all very kind," says Mr Cornetto, "very enthusiastic. All right, we'll give it a try, then."

"*There's* sensible!" cries Auntie Jean, giving him a clap on the shoulder, which makes him swallow his sandwich the wrong way.

"I'll come down first thing tomorrow morning," Mrs Cadwallader tells him, "and we'll get started. I must practise all my old songs. Oh, I'm so excited! It'll be just like old times, Carlo, dear."

The grown-ups embark upon a long chat about plans. Charlie and Ariadne wander off with Lordy to look at the sea. The tide is coming in fast. Lordy, forgetting his age and dignity, gallops about in the fading light like a skittish judge, barking wildly at sea-gulls. They follow him along the tide-line, sometimes pausing to throw a stone or two out to sea.

"She's a bit *overpowering*, Mrs Cadwallader, isn't she?" says Ariadne. "She and that other lady—her sister-in-law, or whoever she is—were having a real old row up at the Hydro this afternoon. In fact, they're both rather bossy, if you ask me!"

"Mr Cornetto doesn't seem to mind being bossed," says Charlie.

"Pretty pathetic of him. You know what, Charlie . . ."

"What?"

"I told a bit of a fib this afternoon to the manageress at the Hydro."

"What fib?"

"Well, I pretended I was older than I was so that they'd give me a sort of waitress job. It's only for one day, to help with the Carnival Lunch. I hope Auntie Jean'll let me."

"Don't see why not. But I can't think why you want to go and work at that old place. I bet they're as mean as anything. They'll probably make you wash up piles and piles of dishes and then not pay you anything."

"Oh, dear. I hope not. I thought it seemed sort of exciting, like the girl in my book who is all alone in the world and has to go and be a governess in a big house."

"Well, don't get in the lift. You might get stuck in

there for ever and not be found until there's nothing left but your whitened bones."

"Don't worry. I won't go near it," says Ariadne with a shudder.

The following morning the portcullis of Carlo's Crazy Castle is lowered, with a notice on it saying "Temporarily closed for renovations. Watch out for our Grand Reopening and Old Time Night on Thursday next!" Inside Mr Cornetto, in rolled-up shirt-sleeves, is already at work rearranging the entrance hall, nailing up strings of coloured lights and bringing in more chairs from the outhouse at the back. Charlie is the first to arrive.

"Ariadne's looking after the shop today while Auntie Jean gets on with the sewing. She's found some smashing costumes and she's altering 'em now," Charlie tells him. "She's got ever so many of them—animal suits and uniforms too, with medals and that. Where's the ladder and bucket?"

Mr Cornetto has put them out ready for him in the Hall of Mirrors, so he gets busy at once. The mirrors are very dirty and fly-blown, and difficult to clean, too, because they are not flat like ordinary ones. He finds that when he has too much soapy water in his cloth, it

slops down the surface and dries in streaks. But he soon discovers that if he wrings the cloth out and lets the clean glass dry until just the right moment, he can get a good polish on it. He rubs away, moving his head up and down now and again to observe his reflection melt from a squashed-lemon shape to dripping candle-wax. From the entrance hall comes the sound of Mrs Cadwallader's voice. She has come to practise her Old Time songs on Mr Cornetto's piano. Charlie finds that the water in his bucket is already dirty. Rattling the handle noisily and whistling, he climbs down the ladder and goes out through the Hall of Waxworks to refill it at the outside tap in the back yard.

As he opens the back door there is a sudden rush of footsteps, and a dustbin goes bowling over with a clatter. He is just in time to glimpse a figure—or is it more than one?—disappearing over the wall. Before Charlie can open the gate and peer out into the back alley-way, whoever it was has disappeared round the corner. Charlie doesn't feel like giving chase. He sets the bin upright again and picks up most of the escaped rubbish. Thoughtfully he slooshes the bucket of dirty water down the drain, refills it and goes back inside, locking the door carefully behind him.

Auntie Jean has just arrived, Mrs Cadwallader has stopped singing, and together they are in the Hall of Waxworks, surrounded by costumes, hats and wigs. Auntie Jean is crawling on her hands and knees round Mrs Cadwallader, trying to pin her into a long dress with a train. Mrs Cadwallader's coat and her long string of pearls are draped over the waxwork figure of Christopher Columbus, who is also wearing a brown bowler hat tilted at a rakish angle.

"There was somebody in the yard just now when I went outside," Charlie tells them, but neither pays much attention. Auntie Jean's mouth is too full of pins for her to answer properly. Out of the side of it she says:

"Mmemmer mime, mear, I mmespeck issa sray hat."

"But it wasn't a cat," Charlie insists.

Auntie Jean removes a few pins.

"If it's those Morgan boys up to their tricks again . . . ! Oh well, they've gone now, I hope. Make us a cup of tea, Charlie, there's a good boy."

"But I'm trying to wash the magic mirrors."

"Can you pull it in a bit more at the waist, Jean?" says Mrs Cadwallader. "My word, this is great! I feel just like something out of 'Upstairs Downstairs'."

Auntie Jean's mouth is full of pins again.

"Breave imm bleeply, mmear," she tells her.

Charlie sighs, plumps down his bucket, and goes off upstairs to the little kitchen where Mr Cornetto does his cooking. There he finds Lordy lurking under the table. Uneasy about all the preparations which are afoot, he has retired from his usual job commanding the pay-box.

"A rotten watch-dog you are, too," Charlie tells him sternly, slamming the kettle down on the stove. "We could have twenty burglars in here before *you'd* notice anything, sulking under there."

Lordy's baggy eyes droop tragically. Charlie relents and gives him the remains of Mr Cornetto's breakfast to cheer him up. As he makes the tea, he decides that he must tell Mr Cornetto himself about the intruders. But when he arrives downstairs with the tea-tray, he hears angry voices upraised in the entrance hall. Peeping round the plush curtain, he sees all three grown-ups huddled together like cornered sheep, confronting the bristling figure of Miss Mona. Her small form is compacted with fury, and she is poking her neck forward like a goose about to peck somebody.

"You're making a perfect exhibition of yourself,

Connie! You must be mad even to *consider* appearing in public dressed like that. Poor dear Caddy would turn in his grave if he could see you—thank heavens he was spared it."

"Rubbish, Mona," retorts Mrs Cadwallader bravely. "I was dressed up when Caddy first met me, except that then it was silver tights. He'd be *glad* to see me enjoying myself, so there!"

"You're far too old for it now—you look quite ridiculous!" Miss Mona tells her cuttingly.

Mrs Cadwallader looks momentarily dashed, but Mr Cornetto puts in gallantly:

"Not at all, she's elegance itself! She's helping to give my place a new look for the Grand Reopening. Excitement, glitter, razz-me-tazz—*you* know . . ."

There is an icy pause. Miss Mona turns her gaze upon him, and he shrinks beneath it.

"I most certainly do *not* know," she says at last. "Neither do I *wish* to know. As far as I am concerned my sister-in-law is making a silly spectacle of herself dressed up like that. I thoroughly disapprove of her being associated with a . . . a . . . ." She looks about as though another stink-bomb were wafting under her nose ". . . *venture* of this kind. It's embarrassing. Take that dress off,

Connie, and come along back to the hotel."

"No, I won't."

"I insist, Connie."

"But I'm having such a good time . . ."

"I'm not leaving here without you."

"You'd better go, Connie," says Auntie Jean, giving her a nudge. "I've fitted the dress anyway. Let's have it back, and I'll go on with the alterations."

"Oh, all right," says Mrs Cadwallader crossly. "But I'm coming back and . . ." She glares at her sister-in-law . . . "nobody's going to stop me!"

A strained silence follows in which Mrs Cadwallader goes off to change. Behind his curtain Charlie wonders why grown-ups have to get so worked up about such unimportant things. He decides that it's not the right moment for tea, so he takes the tray back upstairs and drinks some himself. By the time he comes down again Mrs Cadwallader and Miss Mona have already gone.

"I saw it in the tea-leaves the other day—a dark cloud, a little spot of trouble," remarks Auntie Jean, as she packs up the costumes in the Hall of Waxworks. "Never mind, Mr Cornetto, we mustn't let that Miss Mona interfere with our preparations. Nasty, stuck-up old thing! I thought Connie looked lovely myself, a real picture."

"A picture indeed," agrees Mr Cornetto. "She hasn't changed at all since the old Royalty days—not one little bit. But I'm worried about our Reopening. We couldn't get on without her."

"Of course we won't have to get on without her. As far as Connie is concerned, the show always goes on! Now stop bothering yourself, Mr Cornetto, and try this bowler on for size."

Auntie Jean lifts the brown bowler hat off the head of Christopher Columbus and hands it to Mr Cornetto, who puts it doubtfully on to his own. It is not a good fit. Being much too small, it perches on his head uneasily. He hands it over to Charlie, who, trying it on in turn, finds that it comes well down over his ears and nearly covers his eyes, so that he can hardly see out. All the same, he decides he'll wear it as a change from his peaked cap.

"Good gracious me! Well I never!" exclaims Auntie Jean. She's not looking at Charlie, but at the figure of Christopher Columbus, round whose neck she has noticed Mrs Cadwallader's pearls. Carefully Auntie Jean removes them and holds them up to the light.

"*There's* careless! They're real ones, too! That Connie doesn't seem to care tuppence about all this valuable jewellery her husband left her. Only the other day she left her expensive cigarette case behind, and there were those rings that Charlie found. It's just like her. Once I even caught her using a diamond brooch instead of a safety-pin because she couldn't be bothered to sew on a button!"

"My Mum goes mad when I lose things," says Charlie, "even though she's just as bad herself. You should see her looking for her glasses, or her purse when the milkman calls for his money."

"But *real* jewellery!" says Auntie Jean, and she clicks her tongue in a shocked way. "Well, I shall just have to take these pearls back to my place and put them away safely until I see her again. But I wouldn't be surprised if she doesn't even notice she's lost them!"

"She's a remarkable lady," says Mr Cornetto, "a truly remarkable lady."

Barmy, more like it, thinks Charlie to himself, but aloud he says nothing. Tipping the bowler on to the back of his head so that he can see better, he picks up his bucket and goes back to the magic mirrors. What with one thing and another, he has quite forgotten about the intruders in the yard.

7

The next few days are hard work for everybody, cleaning, sewing, polishing, painting and hanging curtains. The Crazy Castle gradually takes on a new look, and so do the waxworks in their smart costumes, refurbished by Auntie Jean. Ariadne spends hours on a ladder painting up the figures on the outside of the building. She gives the kings beautiful new crowns and moustaches, the queens golden hair and jewels in all colours of the rainbow, and the skeletons grinning green teeth and eyes which glare horribly from their black eye-sockets. Groups of curious passers-by on the prom stop now and then to watch.

"I'd like to do a prehistoric monster—a Diplodocus or a Tyrannosaurus Rex—but there isn't room," she tells Charlie, who is standing at the bottom of the ladder to hand up paint-pots and give advice.

"Even if there was, people would think there were monsters inside and it wouldn't be fair," says Charlie firmly. "Mr Cornetto's ordered two new pin-tables, though," he tells her. "They're arriving today. It's beginning to look great in there."

It certainly is. Strings of coloured lights lend romance

to the entrance hall, where newly-painted chairs and tables are grouped about invitingly. Even Mr Cornetto seems excited. He has put up posters about the town announcing the Reopening, and he is going to accompany Mrs Cadwallader on the old piano, wearing a loudly checked suit and waistcoat and a large flower in his buttonhole. Mrs Cadwallader herself has somehow managed to escape Miss Mona's eye to practise with him whenever possible. But each time somebody has to be on guard in case her small but alarming figure is seen stalking up the prom. So far, all is well. Everybody is in good spirits except poor Lordy, who seems to be more and more upset by all the changes to his old home.

"We'd better take him round to Auntie Jean's, Mr Cornetto," says Charlie on the day of the Reopening. "He can stay the night in the kitchen. Einstein always goes out then. I'll give him a bowl of dog-meat."

That evening the portcullis of the Crazy Castle is drawn up and the lights shine out. Charlie, dressed in a red soldier's jacket covered in medals, has taken Lordy's place in charge of the pay-box. A small crowd starts to collect. They drift inside to play with the slot-machines and gaze at the waxworks and magic mirrors. Then out steps Mr Cornetto, and sits down at the piano. He strikes

up a few loud tinny chords, and launches immediately into the sort of tune that makes you want to keep time with your feet. Now Mrs Cadwallader appears, beaming and splendid in her long old-fashioned dress, and starts to sing. Her voice carries out over the darkening prom. A much larger crowd gathers. There is a certain amount of giggling curiosity. But gradually one or two people start to join in the choruses. Mrs Cadwallader carries them along, coaxing and encouraging. She has clearly never enjoyed herself so much for years.

> "There was I,
> Waiting at the church,
> Waiting at the church,
> He's left me in the lurch . . ."

Business is brisk in the tea-bar. Ariadne flies about in a starched cap and apron, serving snacks. A queue forms for the fortune-telling booth.

"It's a giggle, anyway," says a girl to her friend. "Better than hanging about."

"I had my fortune told. It's much cheaper than over at Penwyn, and she told me I was going to marry a rich rock and roll singer and live in America."

"Those old slot-machines are a real laugh. There's one with a kind of peep-show with old-fashioned bathing beauties."

"She's going to sing again. Keep us a seat over there, will you, Sandra?"

A small party of ladies and gentlemen from the Hydro Hotel pass by and drop in to see what's going on.

"Isn't that one of the guests from our hotel? My dear, I didn't know she was an entertainer."

"I *thought* I recognized her. What's that she's singing? I think I remember it . . ."

"Quite takes one back, doesn't it? Just like the seaside when I was a gel."

"Get us some cheese and onion crisps, Brian."

"Ask her if she knows 'Yellow Submarine'."

"Makes a change from television anyway . . ."

"A week's takings in one evening!" cries Auntie Jean triumphantly at breakfast the following Sunday morning. "Mr Cornetto and I counted it up late last night. It's getting better all the time. Wait till I tell Connie, she *will* be pleased."

"If the Old Moaner finds out she won't like it, will she?" says Charlie. He hasn't forgotten the angry words

he heard between the two ladies when he was hiding behind the curtain.

"No, I'm afraid she won't, Charlie. She'll try to put a stop to it if she can."

"Typical!" snorts Ariadne. "Just when Mr Cornetto is on the verge of gold beyond the dreams of avarice."

"What's that mean?" Charlie asks through a mouthful of cornflakes.

"Rich, of course. I read it somewhere."

"P'raps we'll all be rich. Mrs Cadwallader's really good at making people join in with the singing, isn't she? You'd think they'd be sort of shy, but she won't let them be."

"I wish I could play the piano like Mr Cornetto," says Ariadne. "Bouncing your hands up and down over the keys like that looks so easy, but it isn't really. I've tried."

At this moment Lordy, who has been sitting under the table, bounds out to greet his master, as Mr Cornetto himself bursts in through the back door. He looks very unlike his usual self, with hair on end and shirt tails hanging out at the back.

"Why, Mr Cornetto, whatever is it, indeed?" asks Auntie Jean anxiously.

"Burglars! Wreckers! My place . . . it's been broken into in the night!" Mr Cornetto tells them wildly.

Leaving their breakfast at once, they all hurry round to the Crazy Castle. Lordy rushes inside ahead of them pretending to be a bloodhound, nosing the ground and growling deep down in his throat. The entrance hall is a mess. Tables and chairs have been turned over, a curtain has been half pulled down and is hanging lopsided, paper cups and plates are scattered everywhere, as though someone has been playing a pointless game with them, and nearly all the remaining food has been trodden underfoot on the floor. One of the slot-machines has been damaged and the carved wooden bear is lying on his side in a pool of lemonade.

"The waxworks!" screams Auntie Jean at once, rushing over to the archway. "Oh, thank heavens they're safe!"

"I locked that door last night before I went to bed, so whoever it was never went in there," Mr Cornetto tells her. "They must have climbed in through the little window by the back door. They've been in the Hall of Mirrors, though."

They have indeed. Sticky handprints, splodges of butter and melted ice-cream cling to all the carefully

(80)

polished surfaces. On one big central mirror, written in what looks like tomato sauce, are the words "Thank U Verry Much!"

Looking at it, and remembering all his hard work, Charlie suddenly feels very weary. Then he remembers too about the time when he was polishing those very mirrors and heard somebody in the back yard. Now, too late, he tells them all about it.

"If it's those Morgan boys . . ." says Auntie Jean, but even she is too depressed to get into one of her rages.

"Typical!" mutters Ariadne.

"There's no proof that it's them," says Mr Cornetto. "It could have been anybody."

"I'm sorry I forgot to tell you that day, Mr Cornetto. There seemed to be such a lot going on at the time."

"It can't be helped, boy. Don't you think any more about it. One thing, though. None of the money's gone. I put that where no one'd find it in a hurry. In fact, the more I think of it, nothing of any value's been stolen. They don't seem to have been those sort of burglars."

"Vandals!" exclaims Auntie Jean. "You'll have to report it at the police station, Mr Cornetto."

"Yes, indeed, I suppose I will."

They all follow him back to the entrance hall, where

he stands among the wreckage looking smaller than usual. All the happy triumph of the morning has drained away. Nobody knows where to begin. Only Lordy rushes about, busily growling and sniffing. Ariadne opens the piano and picks out a few plaintive notes.

"Whoever it was never got round to spoiling the piano, anyway," she says. "I *am* glad."

"Well, thank heavens it's Sunday and we're closed until tomorrow," says Auntie Jean briskly. "Gives us a bit of time to help you get cleared up, Mr Cornetto. I'll have to put off Chapel till this evening, but I've no doubt the Lord will make allowances. You put on the kettle and make us a cup of tea, Ariadne dear, and we'll get started."

Mrs Cadwallader joins them just as cleaning-up operations are getting under way. She is in great spirits, and is not at all put out by the scene that greets her.

"I've seen worse," she says. "We had terrible trouble with burglars once when I was on tour. Took all the costumes and all, I hadn't a rag left to wear." She hangs up her smart coat and starts to roll up her sleeves.

"I've given Mona the slip this morning," she tells them gleefully. "She booked us on a coach trip to see an old country mansion, but I pretended I wasn't feeling up to it. She won't be back until late tonight. I'm afraid she's

very suspicious, though. There are rumours at the hotel about what I'm up to here, and she pretends not to hear. I'll be in trouble before long, I'm afraid, but who cares? Give us that scrubbing-brush, Jean. I'll get on with the floor while you re-hang that curtain."

A great Sunday afternoon quiet settles on Penwyn Bay. Cleaning up the Crazy Castle has turned out be an easier job than it seemed at the beginning, and Mrs Cadwallader has rounded off the morning's work by sending Charlie out for a dinner of fish and chips for everybody, double portions all round.

Both children have now been let off for a swim, and are sitting on the beach on their damp towels, Ariadne deep in her book as usual. Charlie is trying to knock a tin can over by throwing small stones at it.

"Having burglars isn't nearly as exciting as I thought it'd be," he says. "Just a lot of mess and hard work. They didn't leave any proper clues we could follow up, like real detectives."

"They wrote 'thank you very much'," says Ariadne, without looking up.

"That's no good. I meant footprints, blood, bits of hair, proper clues like that."

"Well, there were plenty of sticky smears."

"We should have taken fingerprints," says Charlie, throwing another stone and missing.

Keeping her place carefully with a bit of seaweed, Ariadne picks up a small pebble, and, aiming it at Charlie's tin, hits it first time.

"They weren't real burglars, anyway, because they didn't take anything," she says. "And if it's those Morgan boys, which it probably is, you won't want to catch them because they're much bigger than you. It would be completely pathetic."

"I could get the police to send them to prison."

"No, you couldn't. Policemen don't send children to prison."

Charlie is thoroughly irritated.

"Well, I'll do something to them. Give them a terrible fright."

"Don't be *pathetic*, Charlie. What sort of fright?"

"I don't know. I'm thinking," is all Charlie can answer. Ariadne returns to her book.

Later, she says:

"I heard Mrs Cadwallader and Mr Cornetto arranging to go for a walk on the pier this evening. He's going to leave Lordy behind as a watch-dog."

"That's silly," says Charlie crossly. "Lordy's not much good at that kind of thing if you ask me. What do they want to go on the pier for in the evening anyway? They're neither of them interested in fishing."

"Perhaps they're going out together—you know."

"Don't be stupid. They're *old*. Anyway she's always talking and telling people what to do, and all. Nobody could want to go out with her."

"She's got lots of money and jewels and things, even if she is always losing them. Perhaps Mr Cornetto doesn't mind her going on at him. Perhaps it'll be good for him."

"Well, somebody ought to warn him," says Charlie bitterly.

"Perhaps we could make out he's got a wife already, that nobody knows about, like the man in my book. He's got one that's mad, and he keeps her locked up in the attic."

"Go on. How could Mr Cornetto have a mad wife at the Crazy Castle? There isn't room for one. He's packed out with stuff already."

"I suppose you're right," admits Ariadne reluctantly. "Well, they're going out tonight anyway, so if *you* want to give the burglars a fright, Charlie Moon, this could be your big chance."

"What d'you mean?"

"Well they're bound to come back. I read somewhere that criminals always return to the scene of their crime. So you could jump out on them wearing a mask and say 'Boo!', or whatever pathetic thing you're thinking of."

There is a short silence while Charlie considers this.

"All right, I will then."

"What, jump out at them?"

"No, something better. Give them a fright so they won't *ever* come back."

"You wouldn't dare."

"Yes, I would."

"Wouldn't. What could you do, anyway?"

"I'm not telling yet. But you'll have to help me."

"Typical! Why should I?"

"Cause I can't manage it on my own."

"What if they don't come?"

"*You* said they would," says Charlie, turning on her. "You keep talking about all those things you've read about so you can show off. So now we'll see!"

"*All right*, then. We will. Now will you get on with your pathetic plan, whatever it is, and let me get on with this story?"

8

All the houses on Penwyn Bay front, from Auntie Jean's shop on the corner up to the Crazy Castle, have back yards giving on to a connecting alley-way, which is full of old cartons, broken milk-bottles and other dubious rubbish. It's a cat's kingdom, where Einstein haunts the dustbins at night, competing noisily with his enemies for tit-bits. But this evening, at dusk, all is quiet. Not a cat to be seen. The television sets are glowing blue-white against tightly drawn curtains, and only bursts of recorded studio laughter break the silence.

Auntie Jean, after evening Chapel, emerges from the front door of her shop and hurries away up the prom in the direction of the all-night launderette in Market Street, pushing the huge pramful of dirty washing which has been lying in wait for her all week. Soon after she has departed, Ariadne puts her head round the back gate which leads into the alley. Then she creeps out, leading the shuffling hairy figure of a gorilla. It is wearing a long mackintosh and floral headscarf. Almost immediately it trips on a squashed orange, falls down on its face, and has to be helped up and dusted off.

"I tell you, I can't see properly," says Charlie's voice

crossly from somewhere inside the gorilla's mouth. "You're supposed to be leading me, aren't you?"

"All right. You'll get used to it soon. Hang on to me and try not to make such a row."

"It's too hot in here."

"Well!" says Ariadne, pulling him along. "That's typical! It was your great idea to dress up in that suit, left over from some pathetic panto at the old Royalty, and now you're grumbling about it already. I had enough trouble getting you into it."

"It's this scarf on top of the mask. It's suffocating me."

"You have to cover yourself up somehow until we get there, Charlie. Suppose we meet someone?"

"I didn't think this body part was going to be so uncomfortable. It must have been made for a dwarf."

"Hunch over a bit. It'll make you look more realistic."

It had seemed like a good idea to Charlie that afternoon to dress up in a gorilla suit, but now he's inside it he's not so sure. He's had his eye on it ever since he arrived at Auntie Jean's and noticed it hanging behind the sitting-room door. The head part he found on a high shelf at the back of the shop. It has huge grinning teeth, flaring red nostrils, and deep eye-sockets under a shaggy fringe of hair. The body part is made of artificial fur,

zips up the back, and is very dusty. Charlie thought he had managed to get rid of most of the dust by shaking the whole thing out of his bedroom window, but now he realizes he hasn't been very successful. He seems to be hovering all the time on the edge of a sneeze. What's more, it smells nasty inside, and the eye-holes are too wide apart, so he can only see out by squinting down one nostril.

Of course Ariadne was all ready to be scathing when he explained his idea to her, how he meant to dress up and lie in wait at Mr Cornetto's place while he was out, in case whoever-it-was came back again.

"What do you want a *disguise* for?" she couldn't resist asking. "It'd be easy enough without the mask."

But she'd helped him into it and zipped him up the back all the same. She's even admitted that the effect was pretty good. They'd had to hide in the top bedroom until they'd seen Mrs Cadwallader and Mr Cornetto setting out, arm in arm in the summer dusk, for their walk on the pier. After that, it was an all too easy job to lure Lordy from his post as watch-dog with the help of a bowl of dog-meat. Ariadne has "borrowed" the spare key to Mr Cornetto's back door from its usual place on Auntie Jean's dresser. Lordy is, at this moment, very full

and already dozing heavily in one of Auntie Jean's arm-chairs.

They creep along the alley-way and manage to reach the back door of the Crazy Castle without meeting a soul. Once again Ariadne puts the key into the lock, but she finds she has no need to turn it. She had forgotten to re-lock the door when she let Lordy out.

"Hey, wait a minute while I get these clothes off," says Charlie, struggling out of the headscarf and mackintosh. Together they fold and hide them behind Mr Cornetto's dustbin, then they creep inside the house.

At first it's too dark to see anything. They grope their way through the rear door of the Waxworks Hall. The rows of figures stand in uncanny stillness, muffled in their elaborate costumes. A faint light filters through a little cracked glass dome overhead, catching a sharp beak of a black profile here and there, a towering wig, a glittering glass eye. Ariadne finds her throat is dry, clears it, and is appalled by the loud noise it makes. It is much too quiet in here. Her superior attitude to the whole plan drains away suddenly. It seems impossible to speak in the presence of these listening shapes, and even more impossible to walk up the room between them. She flattens herself against the wall.

"Come on," says Charlie hoarsely, dragging her arm and shuffling forward. "You hide up here, behind the curtain over the archway. I'm going to be in the entrance hall."

"It isn't worth it, Charlie. Nobody's here. Nobody's going to come . . . are they?" Her voice trails off into a squeak of fright.

But Charlie is resolute. He pads off into the darkness. Unable to bear being left behind, Ariadne hurries after him, not daring to look on either side of her. She reaches the curtain and peers round it into the entrance hall beyond. She can make out only tables and chairs, neatly arranged after their labours that morning, ready for tomorrow. Charlie seems to have disappeared into thin air.

"Charlie?" she croaks into the blackness.

There is a muffled answer from the far corner. Charlie's gorilla shape is standing against the wall between the big wooden bear and a suit of armour, looking as much as possible like another waxwork figure.

"Hide behind the curtain," he hisses across the room. "We've got to lie in wait."

"But Charlie . . ."

"What?"

"Let's go home after all. I mean, nobody's going to turn up. It's all totally pathetically useless our being here."

Charlie doesn't answer.

"Mr Cornetto might come back and find us here, and we won't know how to explain."

A pause. Then:

"All right. Go, then. You go off home if you like. I'm staying."

"Don't be silly. I won't leave you on your own."

"Well, *hide*."

Ariadne retreats behind her curtain and hides. Charlie stands stiffly in his corner, as much to attention as his gorilla suit allows. Darkness. Silence. Minutes heavily passing. Voices and footsteps are heard faintly from time to time on the prom outside, but they walk on by, and fade away. In what seems like an endless tunnel of time, nothing at all happens. Every now and then Charlie can be heard snuffling inside his gorilla mask. But he is grimly determined not to give in—not for an hour at least. It was his idea, after all.

After a very long time, Ariadne is suddenly aware of a faint thud. It comes not from outside on the prom but somewhere inside the building. She listens, straining.

Then there is another noise, a slight scuffling. Then a door opens slowly. It's the door behind her, right over the other side of the Waxworks Hall—the one she and Charlie came through themselves. Somebody is coming in the same way.

Ariadne presses her hand over her mouth to stop herself from calling out. Has Charlie heard too? Moving the curtain very slightly, and putting her eye to the narrow gap, she can see him still standing in his corner, absolutely still. Behind her she can see nothing at all, only hear the footsteps, creaking up the hall towards her. Now a black shape blots out her line of vision, then another. Two figures pass by, only inches away from her. She sees a shoulder, a bit of anorak, a glimpse of an ear, someone about her own height. They pass through into the entrance hall. There is the sound of stumbling, of knocking into furniture. Then voices, suddenly loud.

The Morgan boys, of course!

"Watch where you're stepping, boy. Want to get us nicked?"

"I can't see. Where's the counter?"

"Over here, where it was before, see? Come on."

"It's breaking and entering, Dai."

"Not if they leave the door open it isn't. That's asking

us in. They ought to know better after the last time, only they're that daft."

"Where's the dog, then?"

"They haven't no dog."

"I've seen one hanging about here."

"Aaaach, come on. Let's get some grub. I fancy some crisps, anyway."

More clumsy stumbling against tables and chairs as they make their way across the hall in the dark. Then a sharp intake of breath. Slowly Charlie's arms have started to move.

"Whassat?"

"What?"

"Over there, in the corner. Something moved!"

Silence. Then:

"Getaway, it's only one of them stuffed waxwork things. We'll soon have that over."

"Not that one—the other! Hey, Dai, let's get out of here . . . DAI! It's *walking*! Aaaaaaaah!"

Slowly Charlie moves forward, all hunched up and hairy, with his arms up and his great mask-jaw poking forward out of its fringe of hair—which is the only way, in fact, he can see where he's going. He's a terrifying sight in the shadowy dark.

The two Morgan boys scramble and blunder against each other in their panic to get away from him. One knocks over a chair, nearly falls, staggers to his feet again, straight into the arms of the wooden bear which lurches forward on top of him. Letting out a yelping scream, he dodges away, so that it rocks and falls. Meanwhile Dai has bolted through the archway that leads to the other small lobby. His brother flees head-long after him. Charlie, arms clawing the air, follows relentlessly.

The Morgan boys now have no idea where they are. They crash about against the wall, knocking into slot-machines, trying to find the other door. Some glass is smashed. Suddenly a blood-curdling disembodied voice speaks right into their ears, repeating the same phrase over and over again:

"Only one person at a time, please . . . Only one person at a time, please . . ." Charlie stops short, momentarily off his guard. But then he recognizes the voice of the "Speak-Your-Weight" machine. Jolted into action, it can't stop.

"Only one person at a time, please . . . Only one person at a time, please . . ."

The Morgan boys are now nearly demented with fear.

Managing at last to wrench open the door that leads into the Hall of Mirrors, they hurl themselves through. Instantly they are confronted by an army of reflections, a forest of themselves, an endless moving mass of arms and legs.

". . . one person at a time, please . . . Only one person at a time, please . . ." mocks the hollow voice behind them. But as they run through the maze of mirrors, more and more grotesque versions of their own faces gibber and leer at them. Suddenly they are brought up short against what seems like a dead end, a huge mirror cutting off their escape. Now, over the shoulders of their reflections, they see the monster that pursues them, with sunken eyes, hairy arms upraised, and awful fixed grin. There's a passage leading on to the left, but here more mirrors surround them, and now there seems to be not one monster but many, great gorilla shapes leaping up, with others crowding behind, all reaching out to grab them.

"Only one person at a time, please . . . Only one person at a time, please . . ." insists the voice in the darkness.

At last another door, and beyond it they see deliverance. The back door leading out into the yard. They see

the evening sky, the ordinariness of the brick wall. With a great burst of speed, the Morgan boys are out of the door and over the wall in an instant, with Charlie still lumbering after them.

Ariadne, left behind her curtain, listens transfixed to the voice of the "Speak-Your-Weight" machine, going on and on until at last it starts to slow down.

"... person ... at ... time ... please ... only ..."

Then, abruptly, it stops altogether.

Ariadne puts her head out and peers through the darkness of the entrance hall at the confusion left behind by the rout of the Morgan boys.

"Charlie?" she calls quietly.

No reply.

She takes a few steps out from her hiding-place and calls again. Still no answer. Charlie has gone. She hesitates fearfully, trying to remember where the light-switch is. She starts to feel her way along the wall, searching desperately. No switch. She finds herself blundering back through the curtains of the archway into the Hall of Waxworks again. Here, at least, there is a little light. But now she is alone with those stiffly posed figures, they appear even more terrifying—Dick Turpin with his pistols raised, the Executioner with his evil axe.

(97)

To get to the back door she must somehow walk the length of the room, exposed to all those glassy eyes. She measures the distance, trying to pluck up courage. She knows that, besides the set-piece of Mary Queen of Scots, there are eight waxworks on each side of the aisle. Head down, eyes on the ground, she starts off. If you look at the feet, not the faces, it isn't so frightening. What's frightening about eight pairs of feet? She counts out of the corner of her eye. One, two, three, four, five . . . nearly there . . . six, seven . . . quick! quick! . . . eight, nine . . .

Suddenly she stops dead, her hand actually on the door handle.

Nine?

That's one pair extra.

Slowly, slowly she turns, eyes still down, and counts again. Six, seven, eight . . . She raises her eyes. Far down at the end of the hall, the end she's just come from, there is a faint rustle. The ninth waxwork is moving.

Ariadne shapes her mouth to a wild scream of fright, but no sound comes out. Flinging open the door, she bolts into the gathering dusk.

9

The lights are on over at Penwyn. The Fun Fair throws
up a harsh multicoloured glow into the sky, and snatches
of pop music can be heard across the lapping water. Mrs
Cadwallader and Mr Cornetto, strolling home along the
prom in the dark, are taken unawares by Ariadne's
sudden hurtling approach. She seems to come on them
from nowhere, blundering into them, hardly realizing
who they are. Gulping and stuttering with fright, she tells
them the whole story.

"That's all right, dear . . . you're safe now . . . never
you mind then . . ." murmurs Mrs Cadwallader, patting
her comfortingly, though she finds all this muddled gib-
berish about gorillas, burglars and moving waxworks
difficult to follow. "What *have* these children been up
to?" her glance says to Mr Cornetto over the top of
Ariadne's head. They both hurry back with her to the
Crazy Castle at once.

Ariadne hangs back, clinging to Mrs Cadwallader, as
they reach the front entrance. This being still locked, Mr
Cornetto produces his key, opens up the portcullis, and
strides in ahead of them. He goes from room to room,
switching on all the lights. The signs of the Morgan boys'

(99)

headlong flight are there all right, but in the Hall of Waxworks all is in order. Nothing has moved. Eight figures stare down at them from each side of the aisle and Mary Queen of Scots bows her neck to the Executioner, just as though nothing had happened.

"There *was* a ninth—I counted," insists Ariadne. "I know it was there. And it did move, I'm sure of it."

But somehow, with all the lights on, it all seems less likely. Even as she speaks, she's beginning to doubt it.

"Well, it was a daft idea of Charlie's in the first place," says Mr Cornetto, locking up the back door. "You should never have taken Lordy away from here. He's a good watch-dog—the best in North Wales, and that's a fact."

"Well, Charlie scared them off, didn't he?—those horrible Morgan boys, I mean," mutters Ariadne. "It was only when I was left all alone in the dark . . ." Her voice wobbles dangerously.

"It's been a long day, love," says Mrs Cadwallader firmly. "We're all tired out. Now come along, we'll walk you back to your Auntie's and you can get off into bed right away."

There's nobody at home when they get back to the shop.

"I wonder where Charlie's got to?" says Ariadne. "We *must* go and look for him."

But somehow her knees suddenly seem to bend under her, and she finds herself slumped in an armchair, hugging the welcoming Lordy for moral support.

"You're staying right where you are," Mrs Cadwallader tells her. "You've had enough for this evening, I should think."

Charlie is hiding in a doorway at the other end of the prom. He had known from the start that he wasn't going to be able to catch up with the Morgan boys. That wasn't the idea, anyway. Dressed in a gorilla suit, it was all he could do to manage a loping stride, which couldn't possibly match the speed they were putting on to get away from him. They've probably never run so fast in their lives, thinks Charlie with satisfaction. They'll be half way to Penwyn by now, and they won't be back in a hurry.

Charlie is so hot inside his mask, with all the running and excitement, that he feels as though he's going to melt. He struggles with it, but somehow it's anchored to the rest of the suit at the back of his neck. Eventually his fumbling fingers discover the top of a zip, and he gives it a great tug. But it seems to be caught. He turns his head

(101)

inside the mask and tries to squint down one nostril to see what's wrong. No good. He can't get round that far. He wrestles again with his gorilla head, sweating and miserable. It just won't come off.

There's nothing for it but to try and get some help. He remembers Ariadne. Wearily he makes his way right back along the alley-way to the Crazy Castle. He daren't walk along the prom for fear of meeting somebody. But when he gets there, to his surprise he finds the back door securely locked against him.

Charlie sits down on the doorstep, his mood of triumph turning to despair at the prospect of being imprisoned in this suit for much longer. He *must* find Ariadne. But then he remembers that Auntie Jean herself will still be at the launderette, which is quite near at hand in Market Street. She could hardly be all that cross with him for borrowing the gorilla costume, after his heroic adventures this evening. If only he can get there without meeting anyone. He searches behind Mr Cornetto's dustbin for his mackintosh and headscarf and puts them on, just in case. Then he sets off again.

He reaches the end of the alley-way and peers cautiously round the corner into Market Street. It's a quiet Sunday evening. Nobody is about. He hurries along the

street, keeping well in to the shop fronts and trying to hide his jutting gorilla jaw under the turned-up collar of his mackintosh. Suddenly Mrs Phillips from the bakery pops round the corner, with a carrier bag full of cakes for her sister up on the Penwyn Road. She runs straight into Charlie. They both stop short, face to face. Mrs Phillips lets out a piercing scream, like a factory siren, drops her bag, and scuttles away up the street, gobbling with fright. Doughnuts and iced fancies roll about all over the pave-ent. Ignoring them, Charlie hurries grimly on.

At last he sees the lights of the launderette, shining out into the street. He peers in through the window. Auntie Jean's still in there all right, idly turning the pages of a magazine while she waits for her wash. Nearby sit two ladies, deep in conversation, and a bored little boy who is gazing at the circular window of a washing-machine, with its whirling clothes, as raptly as if it were a television screen. Charlie edges towards the door, trying to capture Auntie Jean's attention, but it's the little boy who looks up first. They stare at one another silently.

"Mam," says the little boy presently.

"Yes, love."

"Look, Mam."

"Yes, what is it, then?"

"There's a gorilla."

"Oh, yes—lovely. Got your comic there, have you?"

"No, a gorilla, Mam. A real one. Out there in the street." He shakes her arm. "There, Mam."

Both ladies glance over to the door. But Charlie, of course, has shrunk back into the shadows.

"Ooh, a real gorilla. Just like the one on *Animal Magic*, isn't it?" says Mam fondly.

"No, this one's wearing a mac and a scarf thing over its head. But it's not there any more."

"Well, there's unusual. Mackintosh and scarf, is it? Well, I never did."

"I thought it was coming in here."

"I expect it's got some clothes for the wash, then," says Mam. Then lowering her voice to her friend: "He's that imaginative. Always full of fancies—the artistic type, you know."

Charlie, meanwhile, is becoming quite frantic. Auntie Jean won't look up. But the little boy is hanging over the back of his chair, waiting with interest for his reappearance. Now a young couple walk slowly towards him up the street, their arms draped about one another. Charlie, hunching deep into his collar, presses himself against the shop door. But they pass by, far too absorbed in each

other to notice him. At any moment somebody else will, though, thinks Charlie desperately.

At last Auntie Jean's drying-machine stops. She takes the clothes out, spending what seems like an endless and unnecessary time to fold each item carefully. Then she puts them back into the old pram and says good-night. The little boy watches her leave the shop with round eyes.

She is setting off briskly up the street when Charlie looms out of the darkness. She gasps and lets go of the pram handle, so that it nearly tips up over the curb.

"It's me, Auntie Jean," says Charlie plaintively. "I can't get out of this suit."

"Charlie! You did give me a turn! What, may I ask, are you doing out at this time of night dressed up like that? And where's Ariadne?"

"I don't know . . . I mean, I'll tell you all about it when we get home. But please help me out of this suit. I'm so sick of being inside it."

Clicking her tongue with exasperation, Auntie Jean fiddles with the back of Charlie's disguise.

"Drat the thing! It's no use. The zip's all caught up, and I haven't got my proper glasses. I'll have to take a pair of scissors to it when we get home."

"Come on then," says Charlie urgently, pulling her sleeve.

"But you can't walk home like that!" cries Auntie Jean. "What would we do if we met someone? What would the neighbours say? You're enough to give anyone heart failure with a face like that on you, indeed to goodness!"

Charlie decides to keep very quiet about Mrs Phillips from the bakery. Things are going to be difficult enough to explain as it is.

"I've got to get home somehow, Auntie Jean," he says.

Then Auntie Jean has one of her brainwaves.

"I know, you can get in the pram and hide under the washing. I can put the hood up so no one can see you."

"But . . ."

"Don't worry. The washing's bone dry."

"Oh all right . . ."

Charlie feels too tired to argue. Instead he climbs meekly into the big old pram and curls up with his knees jammed up against his chin, while Auntie Jean covers him with washing, careful to see that none of it gets dirty. It's surprisingly comfortable in there. So it isn't only

children who have the really daft ideas, thinks Charlie to himself, as Auntie Jean trundles him home.

Inside the launderette the little boy removes his nose from the glass door and climbs back on to his seat. He starts to shake his mother's arm again.

"Mam."

"Just a minute, dear. Don't interrupt when Mam's talking."

"But Mam . . ."

"What is it, then?"

"That gorilla."

"Oh, your gorilla. Not still here is it?"

"Oh no. It's gone. It went off in a pram with a lady pushing it."

"Oh yes, dear, so it did. Well never mind, it's past your bedtime."

As they pack up to go, Mam says to her friend:

"You know, sometimes I think they watch too much telly. But what can you do?"

10

During the next few days Mr Cornetto is busier than ever before. There are queues every night to get into the Crazy Castle, and even Auntie Jean's shop is doing a brisker trade. Besides local people and guests from the Hydro, parties start to come over from Penwyn, mostly made up of young people, all giggling with high spirits. Mysterious rumours are circulating that the old Crazy Castle really is haunted. It is whispered that strange things happen there after dark, that the waxwork figures hide more than meet the eye, and that lurking beast-like creatures pounce out at you if you're ever accidentally locked in there at night. Even Mr Cornetto himself is the focus of some curious stares and sidelong glances to see if, in spite of his jolly piano-playing and innocent moustache, he has Dracula fangs instead of teeth. The till, however, gets fuller and fuller as the money rattles in.

"Those Morgan boys won't come back, anyway," says Charlie for about the tenth time, as he and Ariadne hang over the rail at their favourite place at the end of the pier one morning. "I gave them a real scare. I told you I would, didn't I?"

Ariadne has been rather quiet since the evening of their adventure, and has found it difficult to go inside Mr Cornetto's Hall of Waxworks even in daylight, let alone in the dark.

"There *was* someone in there that night," she tells Charlie, also not for the first time. "Or else one of those waxworks moved by itself."

"Gerroff!" jeers Charlie, but he relents and adds, "Well, perhaps one did. But how could it? They're just plastic and wire and false hair when you get close up."

"How could *you* know what happened when you went off and left me all alone in there?" retorts Ariadne. "Typical of you, Charlie Moon," she can't resist adding.

"Well, I couldn't very well have stayed behind, could I? A fat lot of good that would have done."

Ariadne looks down at the waves, the colour of a fishmonger's green marble slab, patterned with white foam, endlessly heaving, lifting, and returning to slap the ironwork below their feet.

"Oh, well. You don't have to believe me if you don't want to," she says after a while. "I'm going back next week, anyway."

"So'm I."

"It'll be school again the week after."

"Yeah, worse luck. But better than being at home when Mum's in a bad mood, I suppose."

"I'm going to be a waitress at the Hydro on Saturday, though. Carnival Lunch—remember? I've got to wear this pathetic frilly apron. Why don't you come too, Charlie? The cook's all right. He's a friend of Mr Cornetto's. He'll let you stay in the kitchen. There'll be lots of food left over, I bet."

"Suppose the Old Moaner or the manageress finds me in there?"

"They'll be far too busy at the Lunch. There's going to be a Grand Surprise Bomb."

"An explosion, do you mean?" asks Charlie with interest.

"Not a real one. It's a kind of indoor firework made of coloured crinkle-paper. When you light it, it showers everyone with hundreds of thrilling surprises—paper hats, mottoes and novelties, or so it says on the label."

"Oh. I thought you meant real gunpowder."

"No, silly. It comes from Auntie Jean's shop, and it's going to be the centre-piece in the very middle of the room. It's been in her cupboard for heaven knows how long, and she's pleased as anything to have sold it at last.

There's going to be an orchestra, too."

"Sounds horrible," says Charlie.

"But you'll come?"

"Oh, all right, then, I'll come. Hey, it must be nearly lunch-time. We'd better be getting back to Auntie Jean's. I wish I had my skateboard here—it'd be great on this pier."

They walk back towards the prom, past the iron bandstand with the curly roof which is no longer used, and the rows of empty deck-chairs, flapping expectantly. Only a few holiday-makers are braving the wind, securely wrapped in anoraks and scarves, cheering themselves up with vacuum flasks of tea. Further up the pier are some shelters, glassed in on three sides, with seats back-to-back, separated by a high wooden partition. The side nearest to them is empty.

Charlie takes a run at it, and a flying leap on to the back of the seat, balancing along it as though it were a tight-rope. From this view-point his eyes are on a level with the top of the partition. He can just see over to the other side. There, below him, sits Miss Mona herself! She is so close that he could lean over and pat the top of her neatly waved head.

Charlie is so astonished that he stops still, swaying

slightly and gripping his perch with the soles of his baseball boots. Miss Mona isn't admiring the view. She has her back to him, hunched up and intent on something in her lap. She is putting something into what looks like a large envelope. Then she starts to lick it down. But suddenly as though she senses that she is being watched, she glances up. Her eyes meet Charlie's. In a moment, pushing whatever was in her hands into her handbag, she lunges round the shelter, thrusting her beak at Charlie like a vulture falling upon its prey.

"How *dare* you spy on me, you wretched boy? What do you mean by it? This is the third time I've caught you hanging about and making mischief. And what, may I ask, are *you* doing here?" she asks bitterly, catching sight of Ariadne.

Charlie jumps off the back of the seat and stands there awkwardly, too taken aback to answer. But Ariadne stands her ground.

"I'm sorry if we disturbed you, but we neither of us knew you were there as a matter of fact. We were just going back for lunch."

"Then what were you doing looking over that partition, then, tell me that?" demands Miss Mona, turning back to Charlie. Miserably, he takes off his cap, puts it on

(112)

back to front, removes it and puts it on again the right way round, well over the eyes. He is struck dumb.

But Ariadne answers for him in a clear voice:

"He never expected to see you there, and he certainly wasn't spying on you. So, if you'll excuse us, we must be getting back. We're not supposed to keep Auntie waiting for meals."

And, dragging Charlie by the arm, she marches off up the pier, leaving Miss Mona glaring angrily after them. They daren't look back until they have reached the prom. Miss Mona is still standing there, quite motionless, but by now they are too far away to see her expression. Once out of sight they both break into a run.

"Fancy you being able to get me out of that so easily," says Charlie, jogging along. "I'd never've had the nerve. That Old Moaner just scares me stiff."

"She doesn't scare me. It's only really scary things that scare me. She's just . . . well, typical. And I think she's the one that's acting a bit suspiciously if you ask me, not us."

"How do you mean? She only looked as if she was putting something into an envelope. Perhaps she was sending off seaside postcards to her friends, like we ought to be doing."

"Well, then, why should she get so cross about somebody seeing her?"

"Born cross, I suppose," says Charlie, "like so many
of 'em are."

Auntie Jean and Mrs Cadwallader are reading the tea-
leaves after lunch. Mrs Cadwallader's cup seems to be
extra full of dramatic events.

"There's something really violent here," says Auntie
Jean excitedly. "Looks like an explosion."

"Perhaps it's that Grand Surprise Bomb of yours,"
Ariadne suggests. She is lying on the sitting-room floor,
using Einstein as a book-rest as usual. Charlie is drawing
a monster with Ariadne's felt pens.

"Mona's temper, more like," says Mrs Cadwallader.
"She's really on the warpath these days. She knows
about our little sing-songs down at Carlo's place, of
course. Everyone's talking about them up at the Hydro.
It's driving her wild. She says I'm to stop it, and now she
keeps going on at me about leaving here altogether. Just
when I've started to enjoy myself for once."

"I can't see any sign of a journey here, Connie. But
here's somebody running. It looks as though one person
is chasing another."

"Really?" says Mrs Cadwallader with interest. "Go on, Jean."

"Some kind of a big upheaval in your life. I can't quite make it out. And here's some rings and a necklace, too, very plain."

"That'll be my pearls."

"Well, I hope you've put them away safely, now, Connie," says Auntie Jean sternly, putting down the teacup. "Let these tea-leaves be a warning to you. Fancy leaving them in the Hall of Waxworks like that! And with all these burglars about. It was a wonder you didn't lose them for good, indeed."

"I do try, Jean," says Mrs Cadwallader, carelessly lighting a cigarette. "I know I'm hopelessly absent-minded. But it was Caddy's family jewellery, you know—it's not as though he'd bought it for me himself. I'd take more care of it if he had, more sentimental value. But it just doesn't seem to mean much to me, somehow. The pearls belonged to his mother, of course. Those two rings that Charlie found were hers, too."

"Three," says Charlie, without looking up from his drawing.

"What, dear?"

"There were three rings. I remember."

"Well, I only seem to have got the two now. I suppose
I must have left the other one somewhere since. Oh dear,
don't tell Mona whatever you do! She'll be *furious* with
me. I'll never hear the end of it. She's being difficult
enough as it is. That reminds me—what's the time? I
must fly. She's expecting me."

"I'll be at the Carnival Lunch tomorrow," Auntie
Jean tells her, as she gathers up the cups and plates.
"Special invitation from the manageress, see, as I've
supplied the Grand Surprise Bomb, and the crackers
too. They're my best stock—very expensive ones. I
thought I was never going to get rid of them."

"That crowd at the Hydro are going to need more than
crackers to get them going if you ask me," says Mrs
Cadwallader putting on her coat. "Well, I'm off.
Cheerio. See you at the party. And if Mona's in her
present mood, Heaven help us all!"

11

Charlie is hiding in the Hydro Hotel kitchen. The cook and the chief waitress, Winnie Probert, are prepared to put up with him only if he keeps well out of their way. So he has found a good place for himself between the cupboard where the knives and forks are kept, and the service doors which lead into the dining-room. These have little port-hole shaped windows in them, and flap open and shut continuously as Winnie and Ariadne, frilly-aproned and already red in the face with exertion, rush to and fro. On the kitchen side of the doors all is in turmoil, with Winnie and the cook screaming orders at one another in Welsh and darting about, dealing out plates as rapidly as if they were playing-cards. On the dining-room side of the door, Winnie instantly slows down to a dignified pace, gliding among the tables as though she were on castors, and giving her instructions quietly to Ariadne in English, as they gracefully distribute the half-grapefruits, each with its glacé cherry, to every place.

Now and then, when the manageress isn't about, Charlie can get a peep through the port-hole in the door, to watch the guests assembling. They sit at small tables,

each with a white cloth, a silver vase of carnations, and a cracker by each plate. Most of the Hydro residents are rather sedate, and there are not nearly enough of them to fill the huge dining-room. Conversation is hushed, and in the long pauses in between they look about as though challenging the management to create in them a mood of Carnival gaiety.

In the centre of the room, with a table all to itself, is Auntie Jean's Grand Surprise Bomb, done out in frills of bright pink, yellow and green paper. Auntie Jean herself is in red, her favourite colour. Mrs Cadwallader wears dazzling orange and a great deal of jewellery. They sit at a table with Miss Mona, Colonel Quickly, and little Miss Mellish. The Colonel resembles a trim grey bull-terrier, and he is not in the habit of wasting words. His clipped moustache bristles aggressively as he attacks his half-grapefruit. Although little Miss Mellish does her best to chirp and squeak enthusiastically, conversation is difficult. Everyone is relieved when a musical quartet, consisting of three thin ladies, playing stringed instruments, and one very large one at the piano, strikes up on a platform at one end of the room.

The manageress appears and moves smilingly from one table to another, as though to rally the guests into

enjoying themselves. Ariadne, concentrating hard so as not to drop anything, comes round with the next course—bits of chicken, rigidly set in a kind of yellow jelly, salad and potatoes. Mrs Cadwallader is plainly bored. She picks at her food, and complains that she doesn't like the tunes that the quartet are playing, and says that they haven't any go.

"Ah, you professionals!" cries little Miss Mellish, wagging her finger playfully. "We mustn't forget you're an entertainer yourself, Mrs Cadwallader. I hear you've been having a great success down on the prom . . ."

But, catching Miss Mona's eye, she realizes that she has somehow said the wrong thing, and immediately changes the subject. By the time the trifle comes round, things have not improved. The quartet are fiddling away at a breakneck pace, valiantly trying to fill the huge echoing room with festive sound. Ariadne has been running with trays for nearly an hour, but she has managed to smuggle four helpings of trifle to Charlie in his vantage-point behind the door.

The party at Mrs Cadwallader's table have finished eating at last. Mrs Cadwallader lights up a cigarette in her long green holder, and puffs away moodily.

"I hope you'll forgive me for saying so, but I do so

admire that ring," pipes little Miss Mellish, still struggling to keep the conversation going. "The one with the green stone. It's a very unusual setting, I think."

"My ring?" says Mrs Cadwallader, idly holding out her hand, which flashes with jewels. "Oh, this one, d'you mean?"

"Yes. How very pretty it is."

"That one's been in my poor dear husband's family for many years," says Mrs Cadwallader, taking off the ring and holding it up to the light so that Miss Mellish can see it better. "It's the most valuable of the lot, as a matter of fact."

"Oh, how interesting!" says Miss Mellish, peering short-sightedly.

At this moment their conversation is cut short. The quartet have come to the end of a piece, and play a great flourishing chord. The manageress holds up her hands for silence in the centre of the room.

"Now, ladies and gentlemen, it's the moment you've all been waiting for! If you're all ready, I am going to light the Grand Surprise Bomb so stand by for thrills!"

And with a dramatic gesture she lights the fuse on the big paper confection. There is a hush. The guests, turning from their coffee cups, watch expectantly as the

Grand Surprise Bomb splutters and hisses into life. A bitter smell fills the air. This is followed by some spurts of light, rather like a firework which can't make up its mind whether to stop or start. The coloured paper is slowly turning brown and curling at the edges. Now—*pop, pop, pop!* Some streamers and small objects, wrapped in coloured paper, shoot upwards and roll away over the dining-room floor. Some of the more sporting guests bend down to pick them up, discovering inside some paper hats, whistles and one or two small plastic toys. Miss Mellish unwraps a paper bonnet, which she laughingly puts on, tying the ribbons under her chin.

But Auntie Jean is beginning to look anxious. The smell is getting worse. One or two of the guests are forced to hold handkerchiefs to their noses. Some more coloured lights fly up, and one or two more parcels, but these are steadily followed by a lot of brown smoke, which drifts and billows across the room. The fleeting mood of festivity quickly gives way to one of dismay. People are coughing, their eyes streaming. The manageress flaps at the smoke with a table-napkin, but this only seems to make matters worse. She signals frantically to the quartet, who start to play again, a rousing overture this time. But the guests are retreating to the other end of the room to avoid the smoke, which by this time is so dense they can hardly see one another.

"Quick, get the handyman!" the manageress tells Winnie desperately. "We'll have to put it out, or we'll all be suffocated!"

"The Grand Surprise Bomb's going up in smoke," Ariadne tells Charlie, dashing through the service doors. "Isn't that just too absolutely *pathetic*! And that isn't all. I've just seen . . ."

But Charlie, who has been watching events with interest through the port-hole in the door, has had one of his good ideas. He picks up a huge jug of lemonade, which he has noticed on the table, and puts it into Ariadne's hands.

"Here, pour that over it," he tells her.

Ariadne, who has great faith in Charlie in these sort of circumstances, doesn't hesitate for a moment. She runs back into the dining-room and promptly empties the entire contents of the jug over the Grand Surprise Bomb. There is a sizzling noise, and an even worse smell than before, but gradually the flow of brown smoke decreases, and then dies away altogether, leaving lemonade seeping all over the table and dripping into a puddle on the floor below. The remains of the bomb are now just a mass of charred and sodden crinkle-paper.

It takes time and a great deal of reassurance from the manageress to persuade the guests to reassemble. Two ladies have been overcome by nervous hysteria and have had to be helped to their rooms. The handyman appears with a bucket and mop, and he and Winnie start to clear up the mess. Meanwhile the quartet plays on, one jolly tune after another without a break. But by now the Carnival Lunch is a definite failure. Auntie Jean is trying hard not to catch the manageress's eye. The crackers lie abandoned on the tables with the cold cups of coffee. Nobody has the heart to pull them.

"Now, if you would all like to . . ." begins the manageress, in her brightest voice, but she is interrupted by a loud cry from Mrs Cadwallader:

"Where's my ring?" she says.

12

The eyes of everyone in the room are turned to Mrs Cadwallader.

"I know I had it just before that horrible bomb thing went off and gave us all such a fright," she tells them. "I think I must have dropped it somewhere . . ."

"Oh dear, oh dear, I'm sure it's my fault!" cries Miss Mellish, her paper bonnet quivering apologetically. "You wouldn't have taken it off if I hadn't admired it just now. Then this would never have happened."

At this moment, Colonel Quickly, who until now has not given any sign of enjoying himself, takes the matter in hand. Briskly he declares that the ring *must* be found. With a few brief orders he organizes the guests into a search-party, and a great hunt begins. Every inch of the floor round the table is searched, plates carefully inspected, and coffee cups checked. This proves fruitless.

"Turn out your handbag, Connie," suggests Auntie Jean. "You might have put it in there. You know how absent-minded you are."

Mrs Cadwallader tips out her large handbag on to the table, but no ring appears.

"I think," says Colonel Quickly in a quiet but deter-

mined voice, "that we should all of us, who were sitting round this table, agree to turn out our pockets and handbags for the manageress to inspect."

There is an awkward pause.

"Surely, Colonel, you're not suggesting . . ." says the manageress. "I mean, there's no question of theft, of course."

"A formality only," says the Colonel, holding up his hand. "It's as well to have these matters cleared up right away."

"Oh, yes! I'd *so* much rather we did," agrees Miss Mellish. "I was sitting next to Mrs Cadwallader, and I feel so *responsible*, really."

"Very well, as a formality," says the manageress.

The Colonel is the first to turn out his pockets, methodically placing each item side by side on the table—his wallet, loose change, watch and chain, and a beautifully laundered clean handkerchief. Then it's Auntie Jean's turn. She has no pockets, but her handbag is full of an astonishing number of things—playing-cards, used bus tickets, old photographs, hairpins, bits of a broken electric plug, all come tumbling out. And now Miss Mellish carefully lays out the contents of her embroidery bag, full of a profusion of coloured silks, and

(125)

her tiny purse, only big enough to contain one or two personal items.

"Come on, Mona, your turn now," says Mrs Cadwallader cheerfully. She seems to be the only person in the dining-room to be relatively unconcerned about the loss of the ring, and she, too, has started to enjoy herself. Miss Mona says nothing. She is rather pale. Haughtily she puts down her handbag on the table, opens the clasp, and stands back while the manageress searches through the contents.

"There's nothing here, of course," says the manageress as she hands it back to her. "Thank you all the same, Miss Mona. And now, ladies and gentlemen, I really don't think there's any need to keep you all here any longer. I'm sorry our Carnival Lunch has ended with this little . . . er . . . difficulty. But I have asked the quartet to play to you instead in the Palm Lounge this afternoon—so if you would all care to clear the dining-room . . ."

"Hey, Charlie, you'd better get out of here quickly," says Ariadne urgently, reappearing through the service doors. "The manageress is coming this way. She'll be wanting us to turn out our pockets next, I expect. But don't go away. I *must* talk to you."

"Where'll I hide?" says Charlie.

"There's a little room full of buckets and brooms and things just near the tradesmen's entrance," Ariadne tells him. "She'll never find you in there. There's something I've just got to do, but I'll come as soon as I can."

The guests of the Hydro have mostly drifted into the Palm Lounge, to listen to the music, and complain to one another in undertones about the events of the day so far. Mrs Cadwallader, Miss Mona and Auntie Jean are sitting in basket chairs in a corner of the deserted veranda which overlooks the sea. The two friends are still discussing the possible whereabouts of Mrs Cadwallader's ring, but Miss Mona is very silent.

"I hope it's insured," says Auntie Jean. "The way you keep getting it mislaid, it certainly ought to be."

"Er . . . well . . . as a matter of fact, I'm not sure that it is. I know I should have remembered to keep up the payments, but somehow it kept slipping my mind."

"But supposing it has been stolen? Surely it's a matter for the police?"

"The police? Well, I suppose it'll have to be, if it doesn't turn up."

But Miss Mona suddenly starts to her feet, white-faced with agitation.

"Oh, no, Connie! Not the police!" she says. "I mean . . . think of all the trouble . . . the questions, publicity, even . . ."

"But, Mona, how else are we going to find out where it is?"

"I'll tell you, if you like," says a voice behind them.

They all look up in surprise. There stands Ariadne, still wearing her apron, with Charlie looking over her shoulder.

"And where have you two come from, indeed?" asks Auntie Jean. "And what do you mean, exactly, Ariadne, if we may ask?"

"I know where your ring is, Mrs Cadwallader," answers Ariadne. "It's inside a cracker."

"A *cracker*? What on earth is the child on about!" cries Mrs Cadwallader.

"Yes, one of the crackers that was on your table at lunch-time. And, what's more, I'm afraid I know who put it there."

At this moment a truly terrible thing happens. Miss Mona comes forward with clenched fists, and Ariadne, as though expecting an attack, shrinks back towards

Charlie for support. But there is no attack. Miss Mona simply covers her face with her hands and starts to sob. For a moment they all look at her, quite at a loss to know what to do. But Mrs Cadwallader is soon at her side, with an arm round her heaving shoulders.

"There now, Mona. Come along, now, this isn't like you. Just you sit down, now, and tell us all about it."

Miss Mona collapses into a basket chair and cries bitterly for a long time. In stricken silence, they all wait for her to recover herself enough to speak. At last, painfully, her words come:

"Oh, Connie, the child is telling the truth. I can't deny it. I took your ring when you left it lying on the table, and hid it in my handbag."

"*You* took my ring, Mona?" echoes Mrs Cadwallader, hardly able to believe her ears.

"Yes. Then, when the Colonel suggested that we all submit to a search, I . . . I was terrified. I thought I was going to be exposed as a thief, in front of everyone. So I slipped it into the cracker beside my plate. It was the only way I could think of to avoid being found out. I just couldn't have borne it—but now . . ."

"But Mona . . ." Mrs Cadwallader interrupts her, "I don't understand. Why on earth . . .?"

Miss Mona puts a shaking hand on to her arm. "I'll try to explain. It's so difficult, but I'll try. I owe you all an explanation. I took the ring, and other bits of jewellery too, when you left them lying about. But I'm not a thief! I never intended to take them for myself, Connie. In fact, they're all safely in your bank."

"In the bank? You mean, *you* sent them there?"

"Yes. To stop them really being stolen, by someone else, or from being lost for ever. You were so careless, Connie. All these years you've been wearing the jewellery that Caddy left you—the jewellery that was my mother's, that has been in our family for generations—and I've had to sit by and watch you leave it about, and lose it as though it was so much rubbish . . ."

And Miss Mona starts to cry afresh. Auntie Jean and the children look at the ground, embarrassed by her distress, not knowing what to say. Mrs Cadwallader silently pats her hand for a while.

"Mona," she says at last, "I've been a real pig—a selfish pig! Fancy me not noticing how much you minded about it, all this time. You're right about my being careless, too. Why, I'd have *given* you the whole lot, if you'd only asked me!"

"It wasn't for me to ask, Connie. You were Caddy's

wife, after all. I just took a brooch or a necklace here and there whenever you left it lying about. And when this boy here returned three of your rings, I kept just one, so that I could send it to the bank for safe-keeping, and gave you back the other two—and you never noticed! Then you mentioned—so unconcerned you were about it, Connie—that you'd left your pearls in that awful waxwork place. Heaven knows what might have happened to them there . . ."

"I found them," puts in Auntie Jean. "And I returned them to Connie, of course."

"I didn't know. I thought if I could get hold of them without you noticing, Connie, I could rescue them, too. I *knew* you'd lose them in the end. So I . . . I went down there the other evening when you were all out. I found the back door open . . ."

"That was the night we chased the Morgan boys—" gasps Charlie.

"—and I saw one of the waxworks move," says Ariadne. "It must've been you!"

"Yes, I know I frightened you. I kept very still among the waxworks at first, hoping that you wouldn't discover me there when you came in. I was so confused. I didn't know what to do, you see. But in the end, I thought I'd

better show myself. I was trying to pluck up courage to tell you I was there, but you ran away before I could speak!"

"There! I *told* you, didn't I?" says Ariadne, rounding on Charlie. "And you wouldn't believe me. *Typical!*"

"But now we must get your ring back out of that cracker, Connie, or I'll never forgive myself, never!" says Miss Mona.

"Well, that's going to be jolly difficult," says Ariadne. They all turn to her.

"Why?" asks Miss Mona in a faint voice.

"I knew about it being in the cracker—I saw you put it there when I was being a waitress, you see—and I went back as soon as I could, after everyone had gone, to rescue it, so's I could give it back to Mrs Cadwallader. But it was no good. Because, you see, the manageress had already told Winnie to put all the crackers back into the boxes. And, as they're all the same on the outside, by the time I got there you couldn't tell which was which. So that's why I came to fetch you. You'd better all come as quickly as you can!"

13

They all run to the dining-room. It is empty of guests. The tables are cleared, and no trace of the Carnival remains. They find Winnie in the kitchen, her feet up on a chair, drinking a cup of tea.

"Oh, yes. The manageress told me to put the crackers back in the boxes and take them to her office. Took a lot of extra time, too, as though we haven't had enough for one day, indeed, and me run off my feet as it is."

They hurry back into the hall and knock urgently on the glass door of the office. The manageress appears, rather short-tempered, as though she, too, has had enough for one day.

"The crackers? You're too late, I'm afraid. I couldn't see any further use for them, unless we put them away till Christmas, but that's a long time. So I sent the handyman down with them to St Ethelred's—the children's holiday home, you know. I told him to give them to the children with the compliments of the Hydro."

Miss Mona lets out a wild cry.

"Children? You mean you've given them all away?"

"Yes, I've just told you. They're going back to-

morrow, I believe, and they're having a little party, so I thought I'd . . ."

But her words are lost as they stampede past her towards the front door.

"It's down this way, where the beach-huts are at the end of the prom," says Auntie Jean, breathlessly taking the lead. They all follow her, dodging the holiday-makers through the narrow streets to where St Ethelred's stands, down by the shore. A large expanse of coarse sea-grass and sand slopes down before it and merges with the beach itself. There are no children playing on the dangling rope-ladders, motor-tyres, and complicated structures of planks and brightly painted steel. But their voices, and the sound of very loud music, can be heard through the open windows. They race up the front steps, and ring the doorbell. Nobody answers. The doors stand open. Auntie Jean leads the way into a large bare hall, and, for a moment, they all stand there, panting, at a loss to know what to do next.

At last a student helper appears carrying a large tray full of plastic beakers and sodden drinking straws.

"Crackers?" he says doubtfully, as Auntie Jean tries, not very successfully, to explain the situation in a few clear words. "Oh, yes. But I'm afraid it's going to be

difficult to help you. We've had the crackers. The kids pulled them all after tea. Some of them are still in there . . ." He jerks his head in the direction of the noise . . . "the others have gone down on to the beach."

They enter the big room, where a great many children are bobbing, bouncing, and skidding about on the linoleum, to the accompaniment of a record-player, which is turned up to full blast. Everywhere beneath their feet, amongst the bits of squashed sandwich, sweet-papers, and other party wreckage, lie remnants of the crackers. One or two of them, left unpulled, have been torn open down the middle so that the contents could be removed. All the children have paper hats, and they are all wearing sparkling fake jewellery.

"There was a ring in nearly every cracker," says Auntie Jean faintly. "Rings, necklaces, or brooches, and watches too. Riddles and mottoes. They were my deluxe ones, you see."

Miss Mona covers her face with her hands again.

"Well, we'd better start searching," says Mrs Cadwallader grimly.

Dai and Dylan Morgan are sitting behind the beach-huts—a favourite place of theirs, well away from prying

(135)

eyes. Dai's cheeks are bulging with sweets, which he is popping into his mouth, two at a time, from a paper bag. Dylan is idling with the contents of a large pocket handkerchief which is spread across his knees.

"We've got lots of stuff here—brooches, watches, necklaces, rings, and lots of riddles," he says, rattling them all about together.

"Well, never mind the riddles—they're daft," Dai tells him, dribbling stickily out of the corner of his mouth. "You can throw them out for a start."

Dylan does so, crumpling them all up into a tight ball and throwing it on to the sand. The wind catches it, and scatters the bits of paper among the sea-grass which grows between the backs of the beach-huts and the sea-wall. They have had a very successful afternoon, so far, lying in wait for the smaller children from St Ethelred's and bullying them into parting with their sweets and cracker surprises. Dai is particularly fond of sweet things, but he doesn't care to buy his own as it's so much more fun getting them off someone else for nothing. The cracker things are not so interesting. They have thrown them all carelessly into Dylan's handkerchief, to be examined later, at leisure.

"Hey, I've nearly finished this lot," says Dai, looking into the bottom of his bag. "Time we tried to get some more. Should be easy. Like they say 'easier than taking sweets off a kid'. Heh! Heh!"

Dylan knots up his handkerchief and puts it down on the sand. He eases himself slyly through the gap between the beach-huts. Sure enough, the children from St Ethelred's are still there, some of them playing quite close at hand.

"Here, you!" calls Dai, whistling softly.

One of the little boys, alone with a sandcastle, stops digging and looks up.

"Yeah, you. Got something for you."

The little boy puts down his spade, and, holding on to his paper hat to stop it from blowing away, trots obediently across the beach towards them. Once he is within range, Dylan shoots out a hand, grabs the front of his T-shirt, and drags him behind the hut.

"Got some sweets there, have you?" says Dai, now also on his feet. He throws away his empty bag. Then he tweaks the little boy's paper hat off his head and throws that away, too.

"I've eaten mine," says the little boy, hiding his hands behind his back. "What've you got to show me, then?"

"Show you nothing," grins Dai. "*You* show *us*—what you've got there."

"It's mine. They gave it me. They said we could keep our things out of the crackers and take them home."

"Show us, I said."

"Don't want to."

Then Dai puts his face very close to the little boy's, and says in a quiet voice:

"If you don't show us, d'you know what we're going to do?"

The little boy doesn't answer. He purses up his mouth bravely, to stop his lower lip from wobbling.

"Well, I'll tell you," murmurs Dai. "We've got the key to this beach-hut, see. And we're going to put you in there and lock the door and go away, so you'll be in there all night, see. There's no light in there. And what's more, if we don't decide to come and let you out tomorrow morning, you might miss the train home. And then what will your Mam do?"

The little boy starts to screw up his eyes, which are filling with tears. He brings out his hands from behind his back and offers up, on his wrist, a pretend watch, studded with jewels, with a pink plastic face.

"Let's have it then . . ." says Dai.

But before he can wrench it off, there's a slithering noise, a soft thud, and Charlie Moon drops down from the sea-wall, landing lightly, just beside them. The Morgan boys look round for an instant in surprise, and the little boy takes his opportunity at once. As quick as a flash, he darts round the hut and is away up the beach, running towards the safety of the others, his twinkling legs kicking up the sand in all directions but his watch still firmly on his wrist.

Balked of their prey, the Morgan boys turn menacingly on Charlie.

"What's this, then?" says Dai. "Spying on us, were you, boy? Creeping on the sea-wall up there without us knowing?"

"Yes, I was," says Charlie carelessly. "Looking for you, really."

Dylan's hand has already closed on his shoulder.

"Looking for us, is it? Want to tell us what for, boy?"

"I've got some things to sell. They were given to me, and I don't really want them, but I don't like to say so, you see. Wondered if you'd like to do a deal."

At this last word, Dylan's hand relaxes slightly.

"What've you got, then?" he asks promptly. "Got it here?"

"It's just up at my Auntie's. It's an underwater mask and snorkel, almost new. They're really good—came from a big London shop. My Mum paid pounds for them."

"What d'you want for them?"

"Well, how much'll you give me?"

"Not worth much to us. Don't do much swimming, do we, Dai?"

"You could sell them, though," says Charlie casually. There is a small pause.

"Trouble is, we haven't got much cash," says Dai.

"Not more'n a few pence," says Dylan.

"Spent it all," says Dai.

"Pity. I've got a whole box of stink-bombs, and some itching powder—the sort that really works," says Charlie. "I might throw them in, too."

Dylan can't resist showing a little interest. He picks up his handkerchief and starts to undo the knot.

"We've got some valuable stuff here, though," he says winking at his brother. "Real jewellery, it is. We found it, like. Came by it accidentally, didn't we, Dai?"

"It doesn't look real to me," says Charlie, barely glancing into the handkerchief, which they are holding out for him to see.

"It's the truth. Good stuff, it is—worth a lot."

"Well . . ."

"I'll throw in this 50p then," says Dai, feeling in his back pocket. "Didn't know I had it on me . . ."

"Oh, all right," says Charlie, "I might as well, I suppose. You'll have to come up to my Auntie's and wait outside while I get the things."

Dai and Dylan manage to contain themselves until Charlie has duly fetched all the things he has promised, and they are well out of sight up the prom with them, before doubling up with laughter.

"He swallowed it!" crows Dai. "Fell right into it, didn't he!"

"The way we conned him!" chuckles Dylan. "Easier than doing those little kids back there. It's a good mask and snorkel set, too. We can sell it for a good few quid to Gomer Roberts, the sports shop. And we can have some fun with the other stuff ourselves."

"He must be even dafter than he looks," gasps Dai, tears of mirth rolling down his cheeks. "Fancy him thinking all that rubbish was *real jewellery*!"

Back at Auntie Jean's, Charlie is already carefully emptying out the contents of Dylan's handkerchief on to

the table. Amongst all the glittering hoard, one piece is heavier than the others. The green stone takes the light as he holds it up.

Mrs Cadwallader's ring is safe at last.

14

It's Charlie and Ariadne's last evening at Auntie Jean's. They are leaving on the first train in the morning, and their suitcases are already packed. Mrs Cadwallader, Mr Cornetto and even Miss Mona have arrived for a special celebration supper, to say good-bye. Mrs Cadwallader is quite tearfully sentimental about everything, especially about Charlie, so much so that he is inwardly anxious in case she decides to sing a song to mark the occasion. Even if she does, however, he's in no position to complain. The cash reward she has given to him, and to Ariadne, for their part in saving her ring, has been very generous. On top of this, she has promised to replace his underwater mask and snorkel with the very best ones that money can buy, or anything else in the shop that might take his fancy.

"He's a brave lad—a clever, brave lad," she keeps saying, putting her arm round his shoulders. "Make a good detective when you grow up, you would, an' all!"

"It wasn't all that difficult," says Charlie modestly. "I just spotted the Morgan boys from the top of the seawall while you were all still searching for the ring up at the house. Some of the little kids had told me they were

around somewhere, taking their sweets and cracker presents. I wasn't sure that they'd got your ring, of course. But I just knew I had to get the stuff back from them so I could find out. I couldn't fight them because they're both so much bigger than me. So I took a chance on doing a swop. It was pretending not to be too eager that was the hardest part."

"Wouldn't they be *sick* if they knew they'd got hold of a real emerald amongst all that cracker jewellery and never realized it," says Ariadne.

"Well, I suppose they never will, now, so good riddance to them," says Auntie Jean. "But I hope you're not going to leave that ring lying about anywhere else, after all this, Connie."

Mrs Cadwallader only laughs.

"That's not my worry any more, Jean," she says. "As a matter of fact, I've given all the family jewellery back to Mona. She's much better at looking after it, aren't you, Mona?"

"It's very good of you, Connie," says Miss Mona. "I won't be wearing it in the ordinary way, of course. I intend to keep it carefully in the bank, where I know it's safe. But I do have to thank this resourceful boy here. I'm very sorry about the . . . er . . . unpleasantness

we've had in the past, and I do hope that you'll forgive and forget."

"Won't you miss wearing all that jewellery, Connie?" asks Auntie Jean rather wistfully.

Mrs Cadwallader beams girlishly across at Mr Cornetto.

"Oh, no. I'll still have one ring of my own that I'll be taking the *greatest* care of, won't I, Carlo? You see, I'm settling down in Penwyn Bay for good."

Here Mr Cornetto, who has been very quiet until now, gets to his feet, smooths back his hair, adjusts his butterfly tie, and stands up to attention like a general on parade.

"I think it's now time that I told you all our good news. Mrs Cadwallader . . . Connie . . . has done me the great honour of consenting to be my wife!"

The cries of surprise and joy, hugs, embraces and pumping handshakes that follow this announcement go on for a long time. Even Miss Mona, in her newly relaxed mood, seems pleased. She has been thinking for a long time, she says, of settling down herself in some really *refined* place—in a little flat of her own, perhaps. The conversation falls into an excited discussion of plans—wedding plans, house redecoration plans, plans

for the Crazy Castle, hats and dresses, of course . . .

After a while, Charlie and Ariadne slip away unnoticed. It's nearly dark when they reach their favourite place at the end of the pier. They hang over the rail, looking far out to sea. A little wind is blowing up, and a long ribbon of pale lemon sky marks the place where the sea ends and the huge night sky begins. One or two stars are out already.

"Fancy them getting *married*," says Ariadne. "I never thought they'd do a thing like that. Absolutely pathetic! Still, she was pretty good about our rewards."

"What are you going to do with yours?" asks Charlie.

"I'm putting it into my Escape Fund, of course."

"Escape from what?"

"Well, everything. Being a grown-up and doing boring things and going on about the good old days. I won't need it till I've left school, of course. I've got my wages as well, from being a waitress at the Hydro—the manageress gave me an extra tip for putting out the Grand Surprise Bomb—so it's getting on quite nicely. What about you?"

"I'm thinking about being a detective when I grow up, like she said," answers Charlie, "not a famous actor, as I've been planning. Perhaps I'll ask her to get me a

detective set instead of a new underwater mask and snorkel. I saw a smashing one in the shop where I went with Mum. It had handcuffs, and a magnifying-glass, and stuff for taking fingerprints, and everything. I think I'll go and have another look at it first thing on Monday . . ."

The ribbon of lemon sky is gradually getting narrower. At last it disappears altogether.

"Of course, I might find that I need the Escape Fund before I'm grown up," says Ariadne dreamily.

"It's got false eyebrows and moustaches and all," Charlie goes on. "And wigs, all different colours . . ."

"I dare say they'll come in handy whatever you decide to be," says Ariadne.

CHARLIE MOON AND THE BIG BONANZA BUST-UP

1 Bonanza Blues

It was pitch dark inside. Charlie couldn't see anything except a bit of back belonging to his friend, Dodger Best. They were trying hard to walk out of step. It wasn't easy. Charlie hung on to the belt of Dodger's jeans and stumbled along as best he could but he kept falling over Dodger's feet. Dodger's muffled voice came back to him through the stuffy blackness telling him what to do.

"Come on, Charl. It's like the opposite of marching, see. I lead with the left foot and you go off on the right. Ready?"

"O.K., but go a bit quicker, will you?"

They started off again, one two, one two. Charlie kept remembering a poem he knew:

"Will you walk a little faster?" said a whiting to a snail. "There's a porpoise close behind us, and he's treading on my tail."

There wasn't a porpoise behind them, but an even stranger creature: Charlie's cousin Ariadne, wearing her home-made robot suit. He could hear her breathing heavily as she clanked along.

"Faster, Dodger," he urged.

"I can't."

"Go *on*."

Dodger suddenly quickened his pace alarmingly. Now he was going too fast for Charlie to keep up. They lurched forward, quite out of control. Then, without

(151)

Come to the BIG BOOK BONANZA

warning, Dodger stopped dead. Charlie's left foot tangled with his right one. They swayed about, trying to keep their balance. Ariadne, stepping up briskly behind, cannoned straight into them. There was a great tinny crash, a ripping of cloth, a thudding of wild kicks. Under a rain of heavy objects they all hit the floor.

Charlie was the one underneath. He couldn't even struggle. He just lay there trying not to be squashed to death by Dodger and promising himself never to be the back legs of anything ever again. Especially not a horse. More especially not if Dodger was the front legs. He wasn't a reliable person to go about with at the best of times, what with holding his breath between one lamppost and another on the way to school or suddenly deciding to sidle about like a crab. You never knew when he was going to have a stop-and-go phase. Being inside the same skin with him was a mistake from the beginning, thought Charlie bitterly. Next time, at the very least, it was front legs or nothing.

At last Linda, the children's librarian, wrestling with zips and fastenings, managed to rescue them and get them on to their feet. There were books all over the place. They'd been accidentally knocked off a nearby display stand. Luckily all this had happened in the small room across the passage from the main library, the one where Linda sometimes read stories aloud to them. The door was firmly shut, so the people who were choosing their books didn't rush across to demand who was making all the noise. Even so, Linda looked anxiously towards the door.

"Come on, you three, we'd better get this lot tidied up right away," she said. "Charlie, Dodger, you start piling up all those books—very carefully, mind—and I'll re-arrange them as they were. Ariadne, you'd better get the costumes back into their boxes. I hope nothing's been damaged. The horse suit is only borrowed and I've promised to return it in good condition."

Linda had borrowed the costumes for the Book Bonanza which was going to be at the end of this half-term week. She had hired the big hall which was next door to the library, and there were going to be lots of stands with all kinds of books on them—ghost books and fairy-tale books and books about snakes and racing cars and magic and Egyptian mummies and monsters from outer space. There were going to be badges and stickers and some real writers and artists too. Linda was organizing it all. She had a lot of good ideas, like having some people in fancy dress walking up and down outside the hall with notices telling everyone about the Book Bonanza and getting them to come inside. This was where Charlie, Dodger and Ariadne came in. Today was supposed to be a sort of rehearsal.

"Thank goodness my notice is O.K.," said Ariadne, leaning it tenderly up against a wall. "It took me hours to do. Typical of you to go falling over it, Charlie Moon." She always thought that things which happened to Charlie quite accidentally were "typical". It was her favourite word. The other was "pathetic". Worse still, she'd just discovered another one: "nauseating". "You're absolutely *nauseating*," she would tell Charlie, whenever she could steer the conversation round to it. He wasn't quite sure yet what it meant, but he knew it wasn't a compliment.

They got the books back on to the shelves. Linda looked worried. Her hair was all on end. It was short and curly all over like a red setter that's been out in the rain, only it smelt much nicer.

"There's only a few days to go and so much to do," she said.

"Is Duggie Bubbles really coming?" asked Charlie and Dodger for about the twentieth time.

Everyone knew about Duggie Bubbles because they'd all seen him doing magic tricks on television. He was going to be the star attraction of the Bonanza. Charlie was planning to be a television conjuror too, so he was anxious to pick up some hints. You were supposed to have a top hat, which Charlie hadn't, but he was working on that. He'd also spent his Christmas book-token on a book by Duggie Bubbles himself called *Magic for Boys and Girls*. But the chapter about cutting a hole in a large white handkerchief hadn't been a success because he'd kept getting the hole the wrong size. Mum had been very cross when she'd found out what had happened to all her good linen handkerchiefs.

"Yes, he's really coming," said Linda, "and so is that lady illustrator. They're going to use the platform. Everything's got to be absolutely ready by then. Oh, dear!"

They all liked Linda. She could read aloud ever so well. Listening to her was as good as a play. Dodger sometimes hung about at the back pretending he was doing something else, but really his ears were flapping. They all wanted to help with the Bonanza. But now it was nearly time for the library to close, so it was too late to do any more today.

(155)

They were just finishing tidying up when there was a great roaring noise outside. A powerful engine spluttered a couple of times and then shut off.

A fierce figure appeared in the doorway, covered from head to foot in shiny black plastic, with a helmet under its arm and its face covered like a bandit's with a white silk scarf. But inside it was only Norman, Charlie's young uncle. He quite often dropped in to collect Charlie from the library. This was because he hoped to linger about, chatting to Linda.

Charlie, Dodger and Ariadne ran out at once to admire Norman's big motorbike. Dodger stroked its shiny tank lovingly. Bending his knees and gripping imaginary handle-bars, he pretended to zoom off, leaning over sideways as he cornered at 80 m.p.h.

"I hope he's brought the spare crash helmet so I can have a ride," said Charlie.

This afternoon they were all in luck. Linda had invited everyone to have tea with *her* uncle, Mr Owen Bowen. Unlike Charlie's Uncle Norman, who was young, Linda's uncle was very old. He was often at home and liked to be visited.

Norman was in a good mood.

"O.K., Charlie, get this helmet on. I'll give you a lift round there," he said. With Charlie snug and secure on the pillion, he kicked the starter and revved the engine very loudly two or three times.

"See you there, folks," shouted Charlie above the din, with a careless wave.

The admiring group on the pavement watched as they roared away up the quiet road and disappeared round the bend. Even Ariadne was impressed.

2 A Ghost is Heard

Linda's Uncle Owen Bowen lived quite nearby on the
top floor of a big old house. He was lucky with his view
because his room overlooked the most beautiful river in
the world: the steely, oily, muddy, tidal, glittering River
Thames. The other houses along this River Walk were
mostly very grand. Some elegantly furnished rooms
could be glimpsed through the freshly painted windows.
But the house where Uncle Owen Bowen lived stuck out
like a rotting tooth in a row of gleaming white ones. Bits
of the front seemed to be falling off into the basement
area. The windows of the downstairs rooms, which were
all empty, had bedraggled lace curtains drawn tightly
across them.

Charlie and Norman arrived first, of course, and had
to wait on the pavement until Linda, Ariadne and
Dodger came strolling along the River Walk to join
them. The row of doorbells next to Uncle Owen
Bowen's front door bore the fading names of lodgers
who had all gone away. It was no good ringing any of
them because they were all disconnected, like Uncle
Owen himself. He never seemed to hear anything that
went on down in the street. They had to shout up to the

windows for a long time before his face appeared over
the balcony. Then he dropped the front door key down
to them.

The most difficult thing about getting through the hall
was the smell. Or smells. Was it tom cats, dead rats,
mouldy kippers or simply very old socks? Or all four? It
was hard to tell. Every time they came there the smells
seemed to be different. Today there was an ancient
heater at the bottom of the stairs which smoked and
stank gently, adding to the already over-laden air. As
usual, all the children held their noses on the way
upstairs.

"I'b nod breadigg add all," Charlie told Dodger, scarlet in the face as they reached the first landing.

"Neidder ab I," answered Dodger between clenched
teeth.

"Dawseatigg!" muttered Ariadne.

(159)

Uncle Owen Bowen was hovering outside his room at the top of the house, waiting to welcome them. What a relief it was to be there. Inside, with the door shut, there was no smell at all except for a pleasant whiff of oil paint and turpentine. It was a lovely room. From the balcony outside you could see right up to the great iron bridge with its fairy-tale towers, and the moored barges, and the river slipping past. Near the window Uncle Owen Bowen had his easel and his paints and brushes, neatly arranged upright in big jars. Charlie had never seen so many interesting objects collected in one room. There was the stuffed pike in a glass case, the brass letter-scales, the fourteen old clocks (none of them going), the banjo, the tailor's dummy and the model ship. There were also stacks and stacks of pictures, framed and unframed, not only hung all over the walls but leaning up against them too. Uncle Owen had painted quite a few of these himself. Hanging over the massive sideboard was a birdcage, inside which lived, not a parrot or a budgie, but Uncle Owen's best false teeth and his gold-rimmed glasses. His sight was bad, so he kept them there for safety in case he lost them.

"I've got in some rock cakes for your tea," said Uncle Owen Bowen. "The home help bought them for me."

They ate standing up or wandering about the room because all the tables were too full already to put plates on them. This suited everyone very well, especially Dodger. There was nothing he hated more than a set meal. Uncle Owen Bowen had given them up years ago.

"I like this picture," said Ariadne, pausing in front of the easel. "Are you working on it now, Mr Bowen?"

"Yes, yes. River with pleasure boat. Greens and

blues. Light's a bit unreliable today, though."

"It's lovely. I like the way the clouds are flying up out of the top of the canvas."

"It's coming along, coming along. Must get the paints away before Mr Dix comes. Said he might drop in later, and he'll be ever so cross if he sees them."

"Why *should* he be cross?" asked Ariadne, indignant.

"Mess—paint on the carpet—smells. He complains about the smells. Oh dear, yes."

"But oil paints smell lovely," said Linda.

"Doesn't like them." Uncle Owen Bowen's pale eyes started nervously. His chin disappeared into his neck rather like a goose, which gave him a permanently startled look anyway. The very mention of Mr Dix made him nervous. Mr Dix was the owner of the house. He had bought it with Uncle Owen Bowen in it. There had been some other lodgers too, but they hadn't liked the way Mr Dix had kept popping in to check up on their habits. So one by one they had all packed up and moved out until only Uncle Owen was left. He had lived there all his life and didn't know where to go.

"Mr Dix says that Beauty's making the hall smell," said Uncle Owen. Beauty was his old cat. "But I have to let her go up and down so she can get out through her cat door."

"That old stove down there's smoking badly," said Norman. "Looks a bit dodgy to me."

"No, no. Mr Dix gave that to me himself. Good of him. Second-hand of course but he said it had cost him a lot. Beauty feels the cold terribly, you know."

Charlie knew Mr Dix. He didn't seem like a specially good person. He lived on a barge which was moored nearby, and he was always shouting at Charlie and Dodger whenever they played near that part of the river. Mr Dix had bought Uncle Owen Bowen's house so he could move in himself and do the old place up as a posh hotel. But he couldn't get people to pay a lot of money to stay there if Uncle Owen was messing about on the top floor, painting pictures. Mr Dix kept suggesting to Uncle Owen that he should go into a Home, but he wouldn't. He had an old friend who was in one he said, where the head nurse was a regular sergeant-major. Nobody there was allowed to use a small box of water-colours, let alone oil paints. Charlie wondered why so many things that seemed worth doing counted as making a mess, like practising conjuring, or Norman taking his motorbike to pieces in the front room.

Ariadne asked Uncle Owen if they could see some more of his paintings. She was keen on art. Uncle Owen let them turn some of the canvases that were stacked against the wall face forwards so they could look at them. They were nearly all of the river: on misty days and grey days, or in sparkling sunshine, with boats going up and down, and the water all jumping points of light. They admired them all, one by one.

"Did you do this one too, Mr Bowen?" asked Norman with interest. He was looking at a small chalk drawing hanging on the wall opposite the window. It was of a young lady with dark red hair.

"No, no. That's very old. It's of my grandmother, Lily Bowen. Linda's great grandmother. The Stunner, she was called. She was an artist's model. Drawn and painted by all the famous artists of her time. Stunner was their nick-name for a good-looking young lady in those days, and she was the most stunning stunner of them all."

Linda happened to be standing next to the drawing. Turned towards the light she looked just like the lady in the picture, except that her hair was short and curly and Lily Bowen's was long.

"Lovely," said Norman. Charlie hadn't known until now that Norman was keen on art. He'd never mentioned it.

"I don't think I ever had a great grandmother," said Dodger. "I've got a gran, but we've moved such a lot that I don't see her very often."

"Lily used to live by the river," Uncle Owen told them. "She was a mudlark's daughter."

"What's a mudlark?" they all wanted to know.

"Poor people who used to go down to the river at low tide and search for things in the mud that they might be able to sell. Rubbish and things that people had thrown away. Coins sometimes, if they were lucky. A famous artist saw Lily when she was helping her mother with the mudlarking and cleaned her up so he could paint her."

"Did she marry him?" asked Ariadne promptly.

"No, no. He married someone else. A richer lady. And Lily married George Bowen who kept a pub. But she wasn't happy. Not happy at all, I'm afraid."

"Poor lady," said Ariadne.

"After she died," said Uncle Owen quietly, "her ghost was supposed to haunt the river at low tide, down where she used to do her mudlarking. The place where the famous artist first found her."

They all fell silent, looking at the little drawing. Outside the spring dusk was starting to fall and the colours of the opposite bank of the river, so bright an hour ago, were ebbing away to grey like the tide. Overhead there was a faint scuffling noise, like footsteps walking in tissue paper. They began on one side of the ceiling and worked their way slowly over to the other, paused, then started again, then stopped.

"Who's that up in the attic, Uncle Owen?" asked Linda.

3 Smells and More Smells

There was nobody else in the house at all, as far as Uncle Owen knew. But he had heard that noise at dusk before.

"The place is full of smells and now it's got strange noises as well. I can't make it out," he said. They listened again. Now the noise had stopped the silence seemed ghostly too. Charlie had a nasty chilly feeling in the back of his neck.

"Perhaps it's Beauty catching mice," suggested Ariadne nervously.

But Charlie knew it couldn't be Beauty because he'd seen her sitting on the railings down below in River Walk. He couldn't help thinking about that sad, dead Lily and wondering if, rather than haunting the river mud, she'd taken to following Uncle Owen Bowen about instead. Just then there was a louder, creaking step on the landing and a knock on the door that made them all jump.

"Afternoon, all," said Mr Dix, stepping in without being asked. He was not a welcome sight. But it was a relief, at least, that he wasn't a ghost.

Mr Dix wore heavy dark glasses. When you looked into his eyes all you saw were two tiny reflections of yourself. He also wore a peaked cap which he never removed, indoors or out. It made him look rather like a sea-captain, an idea which he encouraged because he liked standing about on the deck of the safely-moored barge where he lived, pretending he was at sea and bossing an imaginary crew. Very little of his face was visible except for his jutting jaw.

"Good afternoon, Mr Dix," said Uncle Owen, hovering about in front of his easel and paints in the hope that they wouldn't be noticed. But it was too late. Mr Dix was already bearing down on them.

"Sorry to see you've got those paints all over the place again," he said to Uncle Owen, ignoring the others. "I could smell them half way up the stairs, you know. I'm a reasonable man, I hope. Don't like to interfere with tenants. Never did. But this is my property and we can't have oil paint smelling the place out and getting all over the carpet, can we?"

"Not on the carpet," murmured Uncle Bowen, shuffling his feet. "Most careful, I do assure you. A cup of tea, Mr Dix?"

"Haven't time, I'm afraid. Madly busy. Just dropped in to remind you about that drawing."

"Drawing?"

"You know. The little chalk drawing of the girl over there."

"Yes, yes. My grandmother. We were just looking at it when . . . I was telling these young people here . . . I mean . . . Mr Dix is an art dealer, you know," Uncle Owen explained to his guests.

Mr Dix nodded briefly.

"I've managed to get a few pounds for your river paintings from time to time, haven't I, Mr Bowen? I just wondered if you'd decided to sell that little drawing. It's a bad time, of course, but I might be able to find a buyer for it."

"Er, no, I don't think so, Mr Dix, thank you very much. I'm rather fond of it, you see."

"Oh, Uncle, you *can't* sell The Stunner!" cried Linda. "I couldn't bear you to part with it!"

"Pity. I might be able to get quite a good price, you never know," said Mr Dix. "And, considering your rent arrears, Mr Bowen . . ."

"I think it may be quite valuable," said Uncle Owen Bowen, "by such a famous artist . . ."

"Pity it's not signed," said Mr Dix, "that brings the value down a lot, of course. But I tell you what. Let me have it valued for you. I know an expert—a customer of mine—who'll do that for me as a favour. No charge. And there's no need for you to sell if you don't like the price."

"Well . . ." Uncle Owen took the drawing down from the wall and held it in his hands, peering at it.

"I can have it back to you the day after tomorrow," said Mr Dix persuasively. And somehow, before they knew it, he had the drawing under his arm.

"Oh, Uncle!" said Linda.

It was too late again.

"I'll just make another pot of tea," said Uncle Owen apologetically, as he shuffled off into the little kitchen next door.

"You needn't worry, dear," Mr Dix told Linda. "This drawing's quite safe with me, you know, safe as houses. In fact, it's probably a lot safer than with your uncle here, bless him. A dear old soul, we all know, but he's slipping a bit. Memory isn't what it was. Wandering." He tapped the side of his temple. "I've noticed it quite a bit recently. He shouldn't be here on his own, you know."

"I don't think his memory's that bad," said Linda. "He's certainly quite able to make up his mind about selling that drawing. And he doesn't have to if he doesn't want to."

Mr Dix ignored this remark.

"Shouldn't be on his own," he repeated. "I don't like it. As his landlord I feel responsible. Never know what kind of damage he's likely to do now he's getting so forgetful. And he can't look after the place properly, you know. The house smells terrible. I shall be in trouble with the Health authorities if I don't do something about it."

"He's got the home help once a week."

"Well, it's not enough. I wish you'd get him to reconsider a Home. Otherwise I may have to take action. See if you can't persuade him to be sensible, dear—face up to his age." He pressed Linda's arm in a familiar way but she withdrew it quickly.

"Well, I mustn't stop. Can't wait for your uncle to make the tea, I'm afraid," said Mr Dix coldly. "And get him to watch those messy oil paints, won't you?" Without saying goodbye he was off, clattering down the stairs with The Stunner under his arm. They all looked at the small empty patch on the wallpaper where she had hung.

"Perhaps she'll start haunting Mr Dix for a change," said Ariadne.

Dodger was getting restless. All this talk of paintings and people in olden times had begun to bore him. He was inventing a complicated game of hopscotch, using the faded bunches of flowers on Uncle Owen's carpet.

"Come on, Charlie," he said. "My Mum wants me back by half past six. Let's go and play out for a bit."

All three children said goodbye and thank-you to Uncle Owen Bowen before, holding their noses like divers, they rushed downstairs and into the street. It was good to be outside again and take in great gasps of river air. It wasn't dark yet, though some windows along the River Walk were already lighted and encouraging sounds of supper on the way and snatches of radio music floated out into the dusk. Between the street and the river embankment itself there were some bits of garden with low walls and railings. Some had rowing boats drawn up in them, some had flowers and white-painted

seats. The garden opposite where Uncle Owen Bowen
lived was full of weeds and tangled bushes. It had an old
rotting shed which Charlie and Dodger used as their
Club Headquarters when Mr Dix wasn't looking.

Charlie and Dodger started a game called "Fire Down Below". You had to move about without touching the ground, pulling yourself along the railings, balancing on walls, leaping from one gatepost to another. If your foot touched the pavement you were on fire. If it touched three times you were all burnt up. Ariadne climbed on to the shed roof. She was the umpire.

"You're burning!" she shouted to Charlie as he stumbled for a second, just brushing the ground with his toe. "You've lost one life! You're on fire!"

Charlie clung to the railings. It was a very realistic game. He could even smell the smoke. So could Ariadne. From where she was sitting she could see right over the river on one side and all the houses on River Walk on the other. Surely it wasn't pretend smoke she could smell?

It was real, all right. And it was pouring out of Uncle Owen Bowen's front door.

4 Fire Down Below!

"Fire!" shouted Ariadne.

Charlie and Dodger thought this was part of the game.

"Not fair! I never touched the ground," called Dodger.

"A real fire, you pathetic idiot! I can see the smoke." Ariadne was already scrambling down from the shed. Then Charlie realized what was happening.

"Come on, Dodger, quick!" he said.

Together they all ran back to Uncle Owen Bowen's front door. Black oily smoke was billowing out into the street.

"It's from that old stove, I think," cried Ariadne. "Oh, Charlie, whatever shall we do?"

"Better not try to go in there ourselves," said Charlie. "Must tell the others. They can't have smelled it yet up all those stairs. If only one of these doorbells worked." He was pressing them all frantically, one by one, but it was no good. He stepped back into the street. "Hey, Norman!" he yelled at the top of his voice. "Lindaaaaah!" Putting his fingers into his mouth, he managed one of his piercing whistles.

Greatly to their relief, the faces of Norman and Linda

popped over the balcony at once. How lucky that they happened to be out there in the dusk.

"Come down, quick, Norman! The stove's catching fire!"

Norman's jaw dropped. He popped back instantly. Very soon they heard him in the hall.

"Stand back, you kids!" he shouted.

They scattered away up the street as Norman burst out through the front door in a cloud of fumes, carrying the old stove at arms' length. He had thrown a blanket right over it to smother the smoke and stop it from catching fire in the draught and he had wrapped his scarf round and round his hand and arm. He was choking and coughing and his eyes were streaming. He dumped the stove on the pavement and stood well back. After a moment or two he managed to get close enough to turn it off.

Gradually the smoke subsided. Norman collapsed against the railings, mopping his face with his scarf. The situation was saved. The whole operation had only taken a few minutes.

"Is the fire out?" asked Ariadne, scared.

"Yes. It didn't burst into flames, but it was just going to. Lucky you kids called me in time, or the whole house would have been on fire."

"You all right, Norman?" Linda's white face appeared in the doorway.

"I'm O.K. You'd better let your uncle know there's nothing to worry about. But tell him not to have any more old heaters in the house."

"Thank heaven the children saw the smoke. Oh, Norman, you've probably saved our lives!"

Norman only grinned at her.

Norman and Charlie were late for their supper that evening. They'd seen Linda and Ariadne off on the same bus.

Then Norman had gone ahead on his motorbike while Charlie walked home, saying goodnight to Dodger outside the big block of flats where he lived.

Charlie's home was over the shop where his Mum had her hairdressing business. Norman was living with them for the time being because he'd just left college and had come to London to look for a job. He'd been studying something called Philosophy but, although he and Charlie scanned the newspapers every evening, there never seemed to be any jobs advertised for Philosophers. So Norman was being a waiter, part-time, instead.

Charlie's Mum was a bit cross about them being late but she'd kept their supper hot: mince, tomatoes and mashed potatoes. Norman and Charlie were tired out. It had been a long day. They ate on the sofa in front of the television. The programme that was just coming on was a magic show. First the screen was full of silver bubbles and then, who should be smiling at them from it but Duggie Bubbles himself.

"Hey, there he is!" said Charlie, speaking with his mouth full and leaning forward excitedly. "He's coming to our Book Bonanza. We're going to see him real, doing his tricks."

Duggie Bubbles had shoulder-length blond hair and a black velvet suit and he smiled all the time. He seemed to be all teeth and smiles. Smilingly, he amazed everyone with lightning card tricks, pulled yards and yards of silk scarves, coloured streamers and live birds out of a top hat and turned a vase of paper flowers into a white rabbit by whisking a cloth over them and tapping them with his little wand.

"It all seems so easy," said Charlie enviously. "It never works like that when I try to do it."

"Looks as though he's going to do a Houdini act now," said Norman.

Still smiling, Duggie Bubbles removed his jacket and allowed himself to be firmly tied up with ropes and shut into a big wooden box, which was secured with more ropes and even chains and padlocks. Everything went dark, with only a spotlight shining down on the box. There was a tense moment of silence. Then a roll of drums, a loud fanfare of music and the lights blazed again as Duggie Bubbles stepped out from behind some curtains, absolutely free! His hair was a little ruffled and he was sweating lightly, but his smile was as broad as ever.

"How does he do it, Norman?" asked Charlie.

"Perhaps there's a hole in the bottom of the box," suggested Norman. But it had already been proved to the viewers that this was not so.

"I'm going to ask him how he does it when I see him," said Charlie.

"Magicians never tell," said Norman.

5 The Magician Appears

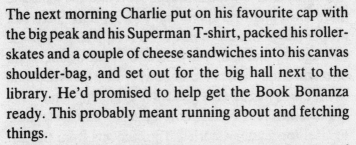

The next morning Charlie put on his favourite cap with the big peak and his Superman T-shirt, packed his roller-skates and a couple of cheese sandwiches into his canvas shoulder-bag, and set out for the big hall next to the library. He'd promised to help get the Book Bonanza ready. This probably meant running about and fetching things.

Linda was in command when he got there, and Ariadne was already busy moving piles of books about. Dodger had turned up too, although he hadn't been asked. This was because he often got rather wild and over-excited at Bonanzas. Strictly speaking, he was also on the library black-list for returning some books late and in a nibbled condition. Dodger had insisted that his dog, Prince, had done it. But everybody knew that no pets whatever were allowed in the block of flats where Dodger lived. Dodger's dog was an imaginary one, who followed him about. The real-life Book Nibbler was actually Debbie, Dodger's little sister. But in spite of all this Linda still had rather a soft spot for Dodger, which was why she was letting him be the front legs of the horse. So she sighed and said all right, if he really *was* going to help she supposed he might as well stay.

There were books everywhere, beautiful new shiny ones with brightly coloured covers, being unpacked from boxes all ready for sampling. Ariadne kept getting side-tracked by one she simply had to read and settled down on the floor with it, where people kept tripping over her.

Display stands were arranged all round the hall, and there was a platform at one end with curtains, just like a proper stage. In fact, it *had* once been a stage because long ago the hall had been a theatre. It had a gallery and boxes on either side of the stage where the audience used to sit. Linda had had the good idea of making some book displays in these boxes. One of them was a Haunted House, for mystery stories. The students from the Art College had made some lovely ghosts and bats and other spooky things out of paper, and rows of hairy spiders on strings. Charlie and Dodger were set to work with a pair of steps, hanging up the spiders. They looked great, dangling all around.

"Pass us up some more drawing-pins, Dodger," said Charlie, perched up astride the balcony rail.

Dodger rushed down the steps, tore about looking for the drawing-pin box, and tripped over Ariadne, who happened to be lying under the steps, deep in a ghost story. The steps wobbled and crashed over, leaving Charlie stranded high above their heads.

"Ouch! Watch what you're doing!"
yelled Ariadne.

"Hey! Get me down!" shouted Charlie.

"Oh, dear, oh, *dear*!" said Linda.

At this moment, who should appear
as though by magic, but Duggie Bubbles
himself! The real thing, in person,
teeth and all. He looked much the same
as he did on television, except that
he was wearing a sparkling white suit
instead of a black one. He was still
smiling.

"Gosh!" gasped Charlie. He swung
himself over the side of the rail, hung
on to a carved pillar and slid down it
to join the others.

"Miss Linda Bowen? I believe you're
the organizer?" said Duggie Bubbles,
pumping Linda's hand.

"Oh, yes. How do you do? We weren't
expecting . . . I mean, this is a lovely
surprise." Linda was all pink and flustered.

"I was just passing on my way to the
studios so I dropped in to see where you
want me to do my act, signing and so forth,
and check up on one or two points," Duggie
Bubbles went on. "Is this the stage?
Small, isn't it? You'll be expecting a big crowd, naturally. I'll be bringing my own equipment and I'll need
proper facilities for it, storage and so on. There'll be full

press coverage, won't there?"

"Oh yes, I've told the local paper . . ."

"I'd rather imagined that the National Dailies would be in on it. And you'll be laying on television coverage, of course?"

"Well, I . . ."

"I usually like—Good heavens! What are those spiders doing up there?"

"The children were putting them up."

"Oh, I see. Great, kids, great!" For the first time he beamed his smile towards Charlie and Dodger. Ariadne, who was skulking in the background, wasn't included.

"Coming along to have your books signed, are you? Bring your friends—all the fans! Only you'd better have those spiders down when I'm doing my act," he said, turning to Linda again, "rather distracting, you know. Want to get everyone's full attention on me, don't we? Now, if you could just show me the stand where I'm going to sign the books. You've got them all prominently displayed?"

Talking all the while, he allowed himself to be led over to where Linda was arranging a display of all his books.

"It's not quite ready yet, I'm afraid," she apologized.

"Well, that's obvious, dear, isn't it? I see you've got *Magic for Boys and Girls* here, but what about my other book, *Out of My Hat*? The one with the big picture of me on the front?"

"It's ordered. We've got a very good local bookseller here and he'll have it by Saturday, I'm sure."

"It's a particularly good one of me. The fans all like

(182)

that one. You'll see that it's laid on, won't you, there's a good girl." He paused for the first time and glanced round the hall. "Bit chaotic here, isn't it?"

"We've only just started to get it ready this morning. Everyone's working really hard."

"Kids under foot don't help, do they?"

"Children are supposed to be who it's *for*," murmured Linda.

"Will you sign my magic book, please, Mr Bubbles?" asked Charlie, inserting himself into the conversation at this point.

"Afraid I've got to rush now, Sunny Jim," answered Duggie Bubbles, glancing at his watch. "Bring it to the Bonanza and I'll sign it then."

"Are you going to get shut into a box and then get out again, like you did on television?" Dodger asked him.

But Duggie Bubbles was already on his way, disappearing down the hall.

"You'll get all this properly organized by Saturday won't you?" he called back to Linda. "I like my personal appearances to go off properly. And it gives you librarians a chance to do something else except sit about and read books, doesn't it?"

"Goodbye, Mr Bubbles," said Linda politely.

"Nauseating," said Ariadne. "Typical. I might have known it."

"He's ever so good on television," said Charlie. "And he's going to sign my book at the Bonanza, he said so."

6 Stuck in the Mud

"Two very rough-looking men called on me this morning," Uncle Owen Bowen was telling Linda. "Kept asking for Mr Dix. I told them to go over to the barge. Wouldn't let them in, you know. Mr Dix wouldn't like it. Oh dear, no."

"Never mind, Uncle. I don't expect they'll come back," said Linda reassuringly. She was only half listening. Worries about the big Book Bonanza were occupying most of her mind.

They were all eating a sandwich lunch in the little bit of overgrown garden between Uncle Owen's house and the river. It was a welcome break after all the hard work they had done that morning. Uncle Owen had set up his easel by the river wall and was painting the view up towards the bridge. It was low tide. The sun was out, lighting up mirror-like patches of water in the black mud. Mr Dix's barge was moored up high and dry, directly in front of them. It was a smart craft with neat curtains in the port-hole windows and potted geraniums on the deck, more like a bungalow than a boat. Uncle Owen kept glancing anxiously in that direction.

"He's found out about my stove catching fire, you

know," he told them. "Made a terrible fuss about it. Said it was all my fault."

"But I thought he gave it to you in the first place?"

"Says I'm getting forgetful. Smells seem to be getting worse too. And the noises. Sometimes I think I'm starting to imagine things."

"Don't worry, Uncle," said Linda, standing up. "I'm afraid I really must go. There's such a lot to do. Why don't you children stay here? I'll pop back for you at teatime."

Charlie and Dodger thought this was a good idea. They were getting rather tired of helping and wanted to roller-skate on the River Walk. The only trouble was that Dodger hadn't got any skates. He had to take turns with Charlie's. They set off, arguing loudly. Uncle Owen returned to his painting. Ariadne stretched out on the grass nearby with a book. Suddenly the early afternoon peace was broken as Mr Dix banged open his cabin door and strode up on to the deck of his barge. He stood there looking at them with his legs planted well apart, like a captain on a bridge. He was clearly in a bad temper.

"May I ask what you're doing on my private property, Mr Bowen?" he called out. "This garden isn't a public park, you know."

Uncle Owen started guiltily.

"Just doing a little oil painting, Mr Dix. River scene, you know. Such a good light today."

"You have no right to use this garden, Mr Bowen. I've told you before. No lodgers have a right to use the garden. It's in the agreement."

"Sorry, sorry. Always used to paint in this garden. Ever since I've lived here. Very fond of the view, you see."

"People will think I'm running some sort of an art school here," said Mr Dix crossly. "Some sort of hippy colony, with that child lying about all over the grass as though it was her own back yard. And is that the remains of a picnic I can see? Really, Mr Bowen, I must ask you to go, and take her along with you. Right away, if you don't mind."

Uncle Owen did mind. He looked as though he wanted to cry. Mr Dix had really upset him. It was humiliating. With trembling hands he began to pack up his box of paints. Ariadne closed her book. Her lips moved silently to sound her favourite word: "Nauseating!" She stepped forward to help Uncle Owen. His big wooden palette, with its lovely sticky mess of colours still wet, and a fistful of long brushes were lying balanced on the edge of the river wall. While Uncle Owen was fumbling with his easel a spiteful gust of wind whipped up from the river. It blew the canvas face down on to the ground. The easel toppled over and knocked the palette, and the brushes with it, over the edge. They lay there, stuck down in the river mud between the embankment wall and the barge.

"My palette! My best brushes!"

This was the last straw for Uncle Owen. He sat down on the wall and covered his face with his hands.

"Now look what's happened!" cried Ariadne angrily. "Please, have you got a ladder or something on your barge?" she asked Mr Dix. "The wall's too steep and slippery for me to climb down, and we've got to get them back before the tide comes in!"

But Mr Dix was stonily unsympathetic.

"I'm afraid I can't help you. They'll just have to stay where they are," was all he said.

"But there must be a way of getting down there!" said Ariadne desperately. "I'll run and fetch Charlie and Dodger."

"No. No good," said Uncle Owen wearily. "We'll have to do as Mr Dix says. Leave them where they are. There's no way of reaching them."

"But you won't be able to paint without them!"

Uncle Owen didn't reply. Slowly he began to pick up his canvas and easel from the muddy ground.

At this moment Charlie was swooping like a gull on wheels up at the far end of River Walk, with Dodger running close behind. They were too far away to see what was happening to poor Uncle Owen. But they were not the only roller-skaters out that afternoon. A pair of slithering figures appeared round the corner, at the other end of the walk: two men, one tall and thin with a sly face hunched into his collar, the other tubby and unshaven. They both seemed to be having a lot of difficulty in standing upright. Reeling, clutching one another for support, hanging on to railings and lamp-posts to stop themselves from falling, they edged their way determinedly along.

"Let *go* of me, Trevor. You'll have us both over."

"Terrible idea, this was, Ray."

"Shut up and try to act naturally. We'll get noticed."

At last they reached the railings outside Uncle Owen's front door and hung there, sweating and panting.

"What do we do now then, Trevor?"

The tall man adjusted his beret, clicking his teeth with irritation.

"We skate up and down, Ray, as I told you. Keep our eyes on the barge. Look as though we're enjoying ourselves."

"This isn't doing my weak ankles any good."

"Never mind your weak ankles. Keep skating."

7 Our Mums Wouldn't Like It

Linda had never seen Uncle Owen Bowen so sad as when she returned at teatime. There seemed to be nothing anyone could do to cheer him up. Charlie and Dodger were keen to try and slither down the wall when Mr Dix wasn't about, but Uncle Owen wouldn't hear of it. He said he didn't want them to do anything dangerous. And anyway, how would they ever get up again? There were no steps anywhere near that part of the river. But he had used that palette for years, and brushes were expensive things. Too expensive for an old man to replace easily. He couldn't hide his distress. All the while, from the balcony outside his room at the top of the house, they could see the river tide rising.

It was getting dark. Time for the children to be going home. Kind-hearted Linda, though she was tired, said that she would stay a while and see to Uncle Owen's supper. Ariadne, Charlie and Dodger said goodnight, but they lingered uncertainly outside Uncle Owen's front door. The River Walk was empty. The mysterious roller-skaters were now nowhere to be seen.

"What are we going to do?" said Dodger. "That palette thing and the brushes are going to be washed away when the tide gets to them. And painting pictures is what Mr Bowen really likes doing, isn't it? Just like we like roller-skating. I suppose he's a bit too old for that," he added.

But even Charlie was at a loss for an idea this time.

"I can't stay any longer," Ariadne told them. "*Typical* of my family to be having guests this evening. They'll go on and on at me if I'm not back in time. And I'm late already."

"You'd better go," said Charlie. "Dodger'n me'll think of something." But he didn't sound very confident.

"Pathetic!" muttered Ariadne. And this time she didn't mean Charlie.

Dodger and Charlie hung about in the street after Ariadne had hurried away to catch her bus. They were plunged in gloom.

"Let's have one more look before we go. See how far the tide's come up," Dodger suggested.

"Better make sure Mr Dix doesn't catch us," said Charlie.

Together they slipped quietly through a gap in the railings into the overgrown garden, and crept through the rank undergrowth of brambles and stinging nettles to a vantage point they knew of behind the old shed. From here they could get a good view of Mr Dix's barge without being spotted. The deck of the barge was empty. But light shone from the port-holes of the cabin. Mr Dix was still at home.

Charlie crept silently along in the shadow of the low river wall until he reached the point, just near the gang-

plank of the barge, where Uncle Owen's palette and brushes had fallen.

He peered over the edge. The light was failing, but he could still see them, lying there in the mud. The river was rising fast. Some other barges further up the river were already gently afloat. Charlie looked about him desperately for inspiration. And just at the end of the gangplank, on the deck of the barge, there it lay: a coiled-up length of rope.

Charlie took his roller-skates out of his canvas shoulder-bag and put them down in the grass. He crept back to Dodger.

"I've got an idea. You'll have to keep watch."

They crept back to the gang-plank. Step by step Charlie edged his way silently along it. The lighted portholes of the cabin were just below, uncomfortably close. He picked up the rope. But with it he managed to dislodge a pot of geraniums, which rolled over on its side and along the deck. Charlie froze. They both fixed their eyes on the cabin door. But there was only the lapping of the water. After a pause, Charlie came softly back, carrying the rope.

Making it secure was a problem. There didn't seem to be anything to tie it to. If only he'd attended more carefully to all those things they'd told him about knots at Scouts. But Dodger surprised him by having a good idea too. He took one end of the rope right across the garden to the railings and wound it round and round one

of them, securing it with a big
knot of his own invention. It seemed safe
enough. Then he tied another knot at the
other end of the rope, took it across to
the river wall and dropped it over. It was
a longish rope, luckily. The end dangled
just a few feet above the mud.

"Our Mums wouldn't like it if they knew
we were doing this," said Charlie.

"But they won't ever know, will they?"
answered Dodger.

Charlie slung the empty shoulder-bag
over his head, gripped the rope with both
hands and scrambled over the edge. He
swung down, then braced his feet
against the embankment wall like a
rock-climber. He closed his eyes for
a moment, hoping that the railing and
Dodger's knot were as strong as he thought
they were. Then he started to lower
himself down, bumping and slithering
now and again, trying to make as
little noise as possible. He could see
Dodger's white face peering down over
the wall, anxious but reassuring. At
last he reached the bottom of the rope
and dropped the last few feet, landing
ankle-deep in black slime.

Uncle Owen's palette and brushes lay just near his feet. He picked them up and, messy as they were, quickly stuffed them into his shoulder-bag. Now came the really difficult bit. Summoning all his strength, he leapt for the end of the rope. His arms seemed to be being pulled out of their sockets as he spun round, trying to re-establish his foothold on the wall. Then came the climb up, hand over hand.

"Come on, Charlie. You're doing fine!" Dodger whispered to him hoarsely.

The way back seemed endless. His arms were aching terribly. Three quarters of the way he stopped climbing and dangled in space, too tired to go on. He was exactly level with one of the port-holes of Mr Dix's barge. Luckily the light which shone out of it just missed him as he hung there against the wall. But he could see inside quite easily. Mr Dix was at a table, bending over something. He was drawing a picture! Charlie couldn't see his face, or what kind of picture it was. But, propped beside his drawing-board, was something that Charlie recognized at once. It was a small chalk drawing, not in a frame, but unmistakable: The Stunner!

Charlie was shaking all over when, with a final enormous effort, he managed to reach the top of the rope. Dodger's hands gripped his arms and helped him to heave himself over the wall. They both flopped on the ground, Charlie still clutching his shoulder-bag, too tired to move.

"You got them then, Charlie?" whispered Dodger presently.

"Yes, palette and all the brushes, I think," panted Charlie, tipping them out on to the grass.

"Great! Bit messy, aren't they?"

"Mr Bowen won't mind. Hey, Dodger, I saw inside that cabin place. I saw Mr Dix, but he didn't see me. He was drawing . . ."

"Perhaps he's another of these artists," said Dodger, not much interested in this piece of information. "Lucky he didn't look out and see you! Let's go and give these things back to Mr Bowen. He'll be ever so pleased."

"It's getting dark. There isn't time tonight," said Charlie, jumping up and grabbing his roller-skates. "My Mum'll be really mad if I'm not home soon. We'd better hide these things behind the shed. We can get them tomorrow morning and give him a surprise then."

"What about the rope?"

They'd forgotten about the rope. There followed a

terrible struggle to untie it from the railings. Charlie's weight had pulled it tight. At last they managed to wrestle it undone. They didn't want to risk creeping along Mr Dix's gang-plank again, so they left it neatly coiled by the river wall. Then they plunged into the undergrowth to a spot behind the shed, a safe hiding-place for Uncle Owen's precious things.

By now it was getting really late. The slick black water reflected the lights from the barges and the young May moon. Charlie and Dodger squeezed back through the railings and scampered away up the street to their waiting suppers. The overgrown garden was full of quiet shadows: two shadows in particular, one long and thin, another squat—Trevor and Ray, no longer pretending to roller-skate, but still watching and waiting. They too had seen what Charlie had seen through the lighted port-hole window.

8 Fishy

When Charlie woke up the next morning his Mum was already busy in the shop, vigorously rubbing up ladies' heads into snowy wigs of white lather. The smell of shampoo came wafting up the stairs. Charlie wondered if she was still cross with him for getting home after dark the night before. She worried about this sort of thing, and worrying always put her in a bad temper. Still, it had been worth it. The first thing Charlie did was to ring up Ariadne and tell her how he and Dodger had got Uncle Owen Bowen's palette and brushes back for him. He made a lot of the dramatic bits, how he had swung like Tarzan over a dizzy drop, which would have meant certain death if he had slipped. Ariadne was furious that she'd missed it.

"And to think I had to spend the whole evening being polite to grown-ups and answering all those questions about how I'm getting on with my 'cello lessons and whether I like my school," she said bitterly: "I couldn't even watch television! It's too nauseatingly pathetic!"

"Meet you at Mr Bowen's house this morning," said Charlie. "We can give him back his things then—give him a nice surprise."

When he rang off he remembered he hadn't mentioned what he had seen through the lighted cabin window. But the thought of it kept buzzing at the back of his mind. It was still bothering him when Norman, who had been working late the night before, emerged for his breakfast. So Charlie told him all about it.

"That Dix character's a bit fishy if you ask me," said Norman, carefully spreading plenty of butter and marmalade on a thick piece of toast. "Linda gets worried about the way he goes on at her uncle all the time. Pretends he's going off his head, which he isn't. Although it would suit old Dix if he did. He can't wait to pack the old man off into a Home so he can move in himself and posh the place up. You can see that a mile off."

"He'd taken that drawing out of its frame, the one of The Stunner, you know, that looks just like Linda."

Norman did know.

"But I didn't know Mr Dix was an artist too. He's never mentioned *that* before. Could you see what he was drawing?" he asked.

"No, he was bending right over it. The Stunner was propped up next to him."

"Fishy," said Norman again, chewing thoughtfully.

"We're going to give Mr Bowen back his things this morning," Charlie told him.

"Think I'll look in there myself. I've got the morning off," said Norman. "Will Linda be there, do you think?" he added casually.

"I don't know. She's busy with the Bonanza. It's

tomorrow, you see!"

When Norman had finished breakfast they went round to River Walk on the motorbike. Ariadne and Dodger met them on Uncle Owen Bowen's doorstep. Together they managed to persuade the old man downstairs and over to the garden.

"It's a surprise," Charlie explained. "We've got your palette and brushes back! Dodger and me rescued them last night before the tide came in."

"Wait there while we get them for you!" said Dodger excitedly.

Uncle Owen Bowen was quite bewildered. He could hardly believe the good news. He stood obediently by the old shed while Charlie and Dodger ferreted about in the nettles.

"We left it just here, I think," whispered Dodger, searching frantically.

"I thought you'd marked the place," said Charlie.

"No, I didn't. It was too dark."

They were getting very scratched and stung. The palette and brushes didn't seem to be where they had left them.

"Come on, Charlie. We're waiting for the surprise," called Ariadne.

"*All right!*" shouted Charlie. He was beginning to get agitated. "It must be somewhere here, Dodger," he hissed.

"Want any help?" said Norman.

Uncle Owen waited eagerly while they all searched. They worked their way right along the back of the shed. With a horrible sinking feeling Charlie began to think that the palette and brushes had disappeared.

"Are you sure you left them here?" Norman asked.

"Course I am." Charlie was in agony. The adventure of the night before and Uncle Owen's surprise seemed to be going all wrong. Already the old man's face was starting to crumple into disappointment, as though this was some kind of cruel practical joke. Norman was kicking the brambles aside. He looked at the muddy ground.

"That's funny," he said. "There's a lot of footprints which look too big to be yours or Dodger's. Somebody else must have been here."

At that moment a whoop of delight came from Dodger.

"Hey, look! They're here!" He was holding up the palette and brushes. "They were in quite a different place to where we left them, all scattered about. I just saw the edge of the palette poking out from the grass underneath this bush, as though someone had thrown them down here."

Uncle Owen was as pleased to see his precious things as though they had given him a hundred pounds. At once he was wreathed in smiles. Filthy as they were he kept fingering them as though he couldn't believe his eyes.

"So *grateful*. So *kind* of you to take the trouble. So *brave*," he kept saying, beaming at Charlie and Dodger. "This must be my lucky day. I thought these were lost for ever, and now I can start another painting. And, do you know, I've got my grandmother's portrait back too! Mr Dix brought her back to me earlier this morning. You must all come up and see her."

Still thanking them enthusiastically, Uncle Owen led them all proudly back to the house and upstairs to his room. There, hanging in her frame in the usual place on his wall, was The Stunner.

9　Very Fishy

"I was *so* pleased to see her again. I missed her almost as much as I did my old palette and my brushes. Now I've got them all back. I just can't believe it!"

"Couldn't Mr Dix sell her then?" asked Norman.

"No, no. Showed it to his friend the expert and, what do you think? He found out that it's a fake! Completely worthless! Not worth more than a few pounds. And all these years I've been thinking it was the real thing. Pre-Raphaelite, you know."

Charlie didn't know. He felt very confused altogether. But Uncle Owen went on happily,

"Of course, my sight isn't what it was. And somehow, you know, I don't really mind a bit. It's a likeness of Lily Bowen, the only one I have, and that's all I care about. I'm glad she isn't valuable. If she had been, I might have been tempted to sell her, you know. And I'd much rather have her here on my wall."

"Well, if you look at it that way, Mr Bowen, I suppose it is a bit of luck," said Norman doubtfully.

Ariadne was silent. But while the others were chatting she stood for a long time in front of The Stunner, peering at her intently.

"I'm glad you've got her back," she said at last.

"The strangest thing of all," Uncle Owen told her, lowering his voice, "is that I've been hearing those noises overhead again. Muffled footsteps. Bangs and thumps. In the evening when there's nobody here, only Beauty and me. It's as though Lily's been trying to tell me something. That she didn't want to be sold at all. That she wanted to come back here with me. Now perhaps she'll stop," he added.

"I hope so," said Ariadne.

Norman said he thought he would go round to the hall and see if he could help Linda with the Book Bonanza, and the children said they'd all come along too. Leaving Uncle Owen happily washing his brushes and rubbing linseed oil lovingly into his palette, they went downstairs. The smells were getting worse. Although the old stove was gone it had left blackened marks on the walls and ceiling, from which bits of old paper hung down in sad festoons. What was left of the carpet was full of holes. A door leading off the hall, down to dark basement regions, lurched drunkenly off its hinges.

"This place is a slum," said Norman, indignantly. "I think Mr Dix is letting it go like this so Mr Bowen will have to move. I keep telling Linda to try and get him to complain to the authorities, but he won't. He's afraid of Mr Dix."

"I wouldn't live here for a million pounds," said Dodger. "My Mum's always going on about the state of the lift in our flats. But she'd have a fit if she saw this. I wonder what's down there?" He peered fearfully down the basement stairs.

"Dare you to go down and see," said Charlie.

"Not likely."

"Go on. I dare you."

"Why don't you go, if you're so brave?" retorted Dodger. At this moment two green eyes appeared in the gloom. They both jumped back hastily. But it was only Beauty, Uncle Owen's old cat. She ran through Charlie's legs, crouched down and regarded them balefully for a moment, and then disappeared upstairs.

Norman went on ahead to the hall on his motorbike, leaving the children to follow on foot.

"You know, there's something very funny going on in that house," said Ariadne as they walked along.

"Mr Dix is acting fishy. Norman said so," said Charlie. And he told her what he had already told Norman, about all he had seen through the port-hole of the lighted cabin the night before.

"He was drawing a *picture*?" said Ariadne. "I thought he was meant to be an art dealer, not an artist."

"Perhaps it's his hobby," said Dodger. "There's going to be a Hobbies competition at the Bonanza tomorrow. A quiz, too, with prizes. I'm going in for everything. The only trouble is," he added, "that I haven't actually got a hobby. But roller-skating's going to be, when I get my new skates. My Dad's going to get me some really good ones. The expensive kind with precision bearings. Much better than your old ones, Charlie."

Dodger's Mum and Dad both had good jobs and earned a lot of money, so Dodger nearly always got the things he wanted. Their flat was stuffed with colour tellys, video cassettes and stereo systems. Even Dodger's little baby sister had her own transistor. But they didn't have time to talk to him much and they never told stories, as Charlie's Mum did sometimes when she was in a good mood. Charlie liked the true ones best, about all the awful things she did when she was a girl.

Ariadne wasn't listening to Dodger. She was thinking hard. She walked more and more slowly, until in the end she stopped altogether.

"I'm going back to Mr Bowen's house," she told them.

"What for?" asked Charlie, surprised.

"Won't be long. See you later," was all Ariadne said, and, before they could stop her, she was hurrying back the way she had come.

They had closed Uncle Owen's front door firmly behind them, as usual, when they left. But when Ariadne arrived back at the house she was surprised to find it slightly open. She walked quietly inside. The hall was empty. Some instinct stopped her from calling out. Instead, she tiptoed over to the foot of the stairs. On the half-landing above her she saw a kneeling figure, his shadow cast up strongly on to the peeling wall. It wasn't Uncle Bowen. It was Mr Dix.

There didn't seem anything else for Ariadne to do but to stand there, watching, unable to go forward or back. Mr Dix was far too intent on what he was doing to notice her. He appeared to be burying something under a floorboard. After a while he stood up and carefully replaced the board, stamping it into place with his feet. Ariadne felt as if she was frozen, like the lady in the Bible who was turned into a pillar of salt, quite unable to move. Mr Dix was about to turn round. Then their eyes would meet. Then . . . But when Mr Dix had finished, he turned the other way without once glancing in her direction. His footsteps went echoing up the three flights of stairs to Uncle Owen Bowen's room at the top of the house. Ariadne could hear their voices, and she could tell by Mr Dix's tone that he was complaining again.

She crept up on to the half-landing. It was easy to see which was the loose floorboard. She scrabbled at it hurriedly, breaking her fingernails on its rough edges. Now she felt like somebody in a detective story, galvanized into swift action. What had Mr Dix been hiding? Something he didn't want anyone to know he possessed. Jewellery, wads of pound notes, a priceless painting? The floorboard came up. She peered down into the hole, then reeled back on her heels.

What Mr Dix had hidden there was a mouldy kipper!

10 Haunted

Ariadne ran straight round to the hall to tell the others all about her discovery.

"Fishy," remarked Norman.

"It certainly was fishy. It smelt absolutely *nauseating*," Ariadne told him.

"Why should Mr Dix want to put a mouldy kipper under the floorboards of his own house?" Charlie asked. "It smells bad enough in there as it is."

"That's it!" shouted Norman suddenly. "Perhaps he's trying to make the smells *worse*, on purpose, so he'll have a better excuse for getting Mr Bowen out."

"That would be typical," said Ariadne. "I'll bet you're right."

"There was that old stove," Norman went on more thoughtfully, "the one that caught fire. Perhaps Mr Dix put it there specially so it would smoke and give him another excuse to complain. And to think it nearly set the place on fire!"

They all looked at each other, struck silent by such villainy.

"There's something even more fishy I've been wanting to tell you about," said Ariadne at last. "I've been thinking. You know Mr Dix borrowed The Stunner, and now he's given it back to Mr Bowen saying it's a fake, that it isn't worth anything. Not by a famous artist at all, or so his expert friend said. But I had a really good look at it when we were there this morning, and there's something funny about it. It looks different.''

"How do you mean, different?" Charlie asked.

"Well, it's really hard to say. But I've looked and looked at The Stunner before—the day when Mr Bowen was telling us all about Lily being a mudlark, you know—and this morning I thought the drawing didn't look the same as it did before. One or two pencil strokes round the edges are different and it's sort of flatter, somehow. You have to look awfully hard to see. Mr Bowen would have noticed himself, of course, but he's a bit absent-minded at the moment."

"He's always forgetting where he's put his glasses," said Dodger.

"I wasn't quite sure. But when you told me, Charlie, about seeing Mr Dix through the port-hole last night, and how odd it was that he had The Stunner propped up beside him when he was drawing, I suddenly thought I wanted to go back and have another look. But I couldn't, because that's when I saw Mr Dix on the stairs."

Charlie and Dodger listened to all this open-mouthed. It was just a bit too difficult to get the hang of all at once.

"Do you mean," said Norman slowly, "that Mr Dix might have been *copying* The Stunner? That he might have given Mr Bowen a fake and kept the real one?"

"Well, he's clever enough to do it," said Ariadne.

"He knows Mr Bowen's sight is bad. Perhaps he thought he'd never notice the difference."

"This is serious," said Norman. "If you're right it's a matter for the police. We must tell Linda about all this. But she's so busy with the Book Bonanza at the moment, I don't want to worry her till it's over. And we can't mention anything to Mr Bowen yet because he gets so anxious and upset, especially about anything to do with Mr Dix. We've got to make sure. We can't go accusing anybody of anything until we've got absolute proof. Now remember, you lot, not a word to anyone for the moment until I can think what to do."

They all promised.

"Fancy all this fuss about a little chalk drawing," Dodger said to Charlie later, as they were humping books about. "My Mum puts all my drawings in the bin."

"You've got to get famous or dead before they're valuable," Charlie told him.

"Well, even if I was both, it won't do me any good if the binman's got them," said Dodger bitterly. "My baby sister usually nibbles them round the edges, too. I don't suppose even that famous artist our teacher was telling us about— you know, the very thin chap, Lean Ardo what's-his-name . . ."

"Da Vinci, I think. The one who tried to invent wings."

"Yes, him. Well, I don't suppose even *he* could have got to be such a famous artist with my Mum and sister around."

"Perhaps he didn't have a Mum, or a sister. Perhaps he could just stay at home all day and paint pictures and invent things."

"Must have been great. Even if he did get thin with nobody to cook his dinners."

That evening, after supper, Norman couldn't settle down to anything. He paced restlessly up and down the sitting-room, frowning deeply and nibbling potato crisps. They helped him to think.

"I'm going for a walk down to the river. Maybe have a chat with Mr Bowen," he said at last.

"Can I come?" asked Charlie promptly.

"It's too late for you to be going out," said Mum, looking sternly round her newspaper. "You've got a big day tomorrow at the Book Bonanza. I'm not having you up till all hours, getting tired out, even if it is half-term."

"But I'm not getting tired out. I'm not in the least bit tired," Charlie protested. "*Please*, Mum. I'll be with Norman."

"We won't be long," Norman said.

Mum wavered for a second and Charlie, taking up the advantage with a skill born of long experience, was already putting on his anorak.

"You've got to be in bed by nine," Mum called out after him as he and Norman ran downstairs.

It was dark now. Down on the River
Walk the old-fashioned street-lamps were
already lit. There were very few people
about, only a few strollers on their way
to the pub on the corner. Uncle Owen Bowen's
house was shrouded in darkness. Norman and
Charlie stood in the street, looking up at
his window, but the light was out.

"Must have gone to bed already," said
Norman. "We'd better not disturb him. I
wanted to get another look at The Stunner
but it'll have to wait till tomorrow, I
suppose."

They retreated to the other side of the
street and leant against the garden railings
in the shadow of a straggling elder bush,
smelling the night river smells and wondering what to do next. Just then a familiar
figure turned the corner and walked briskly
up the street towards them—peaked cap,
dark glasses, jutting jaw. Mr Dix himself!

Norman and Charlie instinctively
drew back into the shadow. Mr Dix
hadn't seen them. He stopped under
a street-lamp, glancing up at
the house. After a moment he
felt in his pocket, produced
a key, and let himself in.

Norman and Charlie waited and watched. No lights appeared in the windows. The house remained as black and silent as before. After a while they could see a pale light, a torch or a candle perhaps, appearing fitfully on the first floor landing. It disappeared, then reappeared, moving from room to room.

"Is he burying another kipper, do you think?" whispered Charlie. "Why doesn't he put the lights on?"

"Perhaps he doesn't want Mr Bowen to know he's there," answered Norman.

The house went quite dark again. Then, eerily, the light appeared once more, this time in one of the three tiny attic windows above Uncle Owen's room, the attic that was supposed always to be empty. It started to move across the breadth of the house and back again, showing in one window then another. Up and down, up and down, like a ghost walking. Suddenly Mr Dix's profile was thrown up quite sharply against the pane, slightly distorted, like an evil caricature of the man inside. Then the light went out.

Charlie moved closer to Norman. He was very glad that he hadn't come there alone.

"It's scary. Do you think Mr Bowen's awake?"

"No wonder he feels haunted," muttered Norman. "But it's not the ghost of Lily Bowen who's doing the haunting. It's Mr Dix."

"I'd put my head under the blankets if I was in there," said Charlie. But Norman was furiously angry.

"He ought to be had up, frightening an old man like that. It's downright cruel."

"Perhaps he's coming down again," said Charlie. "He'd better not catch us here watching the house."

"Things are fitting together like a jigsaw puzzle," said Norman. "Come on, Charlie, we'd better be going home. I've got to think."

But another piece of the jigsaw, unknown to Norman, was close at hand. They were not the only watchers on the River Walk that night. Two pairs of eyes followed them as they hurried away under the lamplight. Trevor and Ray, crouched in the rank grass of the overgrown garden, stirred stiffly in their hiding place as they watched them out of sight.

11 Dark Doings

"I thought they'd never go," said Ray. "Thought we were stuck here in this blooming grass like a couple of broody swans. Ooo, my leg's gone to sleep."

"Get up, quick. We've got to get going. Wasted enough time as it is," snapped Trevor.

"It's too late, man. Dix is over at the house. He might be back any minute."

"It's our last chance, isn't it? You want to be in on this deal, don't you?"

"Yes, Trevor."

"Well, come *on*, then."

They started to move like two bobbing shadows along the river wall towards the gang-plank of the barge.

"I can't feel my leg at all," whispered Ray, bent double.

"You and your leg. It's always something with you. We wasted all yesterday messing about on those roller-skates with you complaining about your bruises. Then you had to go and sit on that old palette when we were hiding behind the shed and get colours all over the seat of your trousers."

"Wish I hadn't thrown that thing into the bushes now. Might have been worth a bob or two. Brushes too."

"A few bob!" spat Trevor scornfully.

They reached the gang-plank and paused there, eyeing the cabin door. The port-holes were dark. The tide was coming in, and the barge was already lifting on the lapping water. There was no other sound or movement.

"You're sure he's still got the drawing in there?"

"Yeah, sure. We saw him doing the copy, didn't we? And we've been watching him ever since. He hasn't left the barge except to go over to the house. But he's one of the quickest workers in the business. He'll be getting rid of it like a hot potato, tomorrow probably. He's been putting out feelers already, trying to see what kind of price he can get for it from a crooked dealer."

Ray giggled. "You ought to know all about *that*," he said.

"Quick, before he gets here. That cabin door's probably locked but I can get it open in no time. You stay on deck and keep watch."

Trevor hopped silently on to the gang-plank and padded along it like a lean cat. Ray followed, making the boards bend and creak. Together, they were outlined sharply against the sky. Trevor landed lightly on the deck. Ray paused, balancing uneasily.

"You two want something?" said a clear voice suddenly from the bank behind him.

Ray leapt into the air, spun round, and crashed down again with knees bent. The gang-plank groaned. Mr Dix stood there blocking the way. His sun-glasses gleamed menacingly in the darkness like the eyes of a large insect. He seemed to have appeared out of nowhere.

"Gas Board!" cried Ray. "We're from the Gas Board—"

"At this time of night?" Mr Dix took a step forward.

"Just checking. Looking for a leak. Trevor—we've done it wrong again, Trevor—Trevaaaaah . . ."

Trevor reacted more directly. At the sound of Mr Dix's voice he leapt back on to the gang-plank and sprinted along it, cannoning into Ray and throwing him completely off-balance. Locked together, they waltzed wildly. Then Trevor jerked himself free. Reaching the bank, he met Mr Dix head on. For a few dangerous moments they grappled silently.

Ray struggled to keep his footing on the gang-plank, arms out, beating the air like wings. Then he toppled slowly sideways and disappeared from view. A huge splash followed as he hit four feet of water between the barge and the river wall.

Meanwhile Trevor had managed to heave Mr Dix into an elder bush where he collapsed heavily backwards into the headily-scented flowers. Seizing his chance, Trevor tore across the garden and, taking the railings like a hurdler, was away up the deserted street.

"Get him! Stop him, can't you?" roared Mr Dix, but nobody heard. He fought his way out of the bush and began to give chase, shedding white blossoms behind him. Unable to jump the railings, he used some regrettably ugly language as he fumbled with the gate.

By this time Ray had surfaced in the river and was staggering about, spewing dirty water and shouting to Trevor to get him out. But Trevor was already well out of earshot.

Charlie and Norman were on their way home up one of the narrow streets which led away from the river. They heard the cries echoing distantly from River Walk, then swift footsteps running up the street behind them. Norman glanced round, surprised. Then he gripped Charlie's arm.

"Seems to be somebody chasing us. Quick, Charlie. Better be on the safe side. Can you make it to the corner, double quick, do you think?"

Charlie obediently broke into a jog-trot. They could hear Trevor gasping and heaving for breath as he loped up behind them. Norman and Charlie quickened their pace to a run. Trevor was gaining on them. They were nearly at the corner, where the brighter street lights shone, when he drew level with them. Ahead they could see a bus just pulling away from the kerb. Trevor shoved his way violently between them, sending Charlie reeling against the wall, and ran on into the main road. For a moment or two he sprinted level with the moving bus. As it accelerated he put on a desperate spurt and took a flying leap on to the platform. He nearly missed his footing but the conductor caught his arm and hauled him aboard. They saw his white face looking back at them before he disappeared up the stairs.

"*He* was in a bit of a hurry," said Norman. "You all right, Charlie?"

Winded, Charlie was leaning against the wall.

"He didn't half give me a shove," he said, rubbing his elbow. "Worse than the dinner queue at school."

"Must have been his last bus. I'm glad he wasn't chasing us, anyway," said Norman. He took Charlie's arm. "We've got to get you home. Your Mum said nine o'clock, and there'll be terrible trouble if we're late."

But before Charlie could collect himself another flying figure came up the street behind them. It was Ray, oozing water, his clothes flapping desperately about him. He lolloped towards them like a creature risen out of the primeval mud.

"Trevor, wait for me," he was shouting, "Trevaaaah . . ."

Charlie was flung against the wall a second time as he plunged past. Reaching the corner, Ray paused for a moment, moaning, then ran off in the direction of the vanishing bus. Norman helped Charlie to his feet for a second time.

"Nutter night," he said. "They're everywhere. It'll be Things from Outer Space next. Come on, Charl."

They were just turning into the main road when somebody, walking briskly in the other direction, bumped straight into them. For the third time that evening Charlie was nearly knocked off his feet.

"Sorry," said the man briefly, hardly bothering to stop. He didn't recognize Charlie, but Charlie recognized him.

"Hey, Norman, do you know who that was?" he said, staring after him in surprise.

Norman was in no mood for guessing.

"The Incredible Hulk, of course," he said, dragging Charlie forward by the arm. Charlie allowed himself to be dragged, but he was still looking back over his shoulder.

"Didn't you see?" he said excitedly. "It was Duggie Bubbles! I know it was. I saw him quite close up at the hall yesterday. I wonder what he's doing down here?"

"Another disappearing act, probably," answered Norman, striding purposefully homewards.

12 Bonanza Day

Charlie woke up the next morning still thinking about Duggie Bubbles. He had been dreaming that he was sitting on the lid of a box, trying to keep it shut, while Duggie Bubbles, who was inside, kept trying to jump out like a jack-in-the-box. Later in the dream Charlie found himself trying to do magic tricks before a huge audience, but everything he did kept going wrong. Now, fully awake, he remembered it was Bonanza day, and it was late already.

He hurried out of bed and searched about for his favourite book. It was extra large and brightly coloured: *Magic for Boys and Girls*. He was beginning to think that seeing Duggie Bubbles on the way home last night had all been part of his dream. But he was determined to get his book signed at the Bonanza. Mum had told him that signed books were sometimes valuable. He had written his own name already, in bold writing on the fly-leaf: "This Book Belongs to Chas. L. G. Moon." That signature was going to be famous too, he was quite sure.

The first thing he saw when he reached the hall was Ariadne, already encased in her robot suit, walking up and down on the steps in front of the main entrance. She

had a blue light on her head which flashed on and off when she pressed a button inside. The Bonanza hadn't opened yet but already quite a few people had collected and were watching her with curiosity.

"Where's Dodger?" Charlie shouted into one of her small coffee-strainer ears.

"Round the back," came Ariadne's voice, rather muffled, from inside. "He's getting into his half of the horse. Linda's there too. You'd better hurry."

Charlie couldn't resist giving a few raps on her plastic casing. Ariadne flashed her light at him fiercely. Secretly he was rather jealous. Being inside a robot seemed much more fun than the back legs of a horse. He had tried to talk Dodger into letting him be the front part, but it hadn't worked. When Charlie found him in the dressing-room place behind the hall he had already got the head on. The front legs were crumpled round his ankles like concertinas.

"Hee-haw, hee-haw!" he went when he saw Charlie, clattering the huge set of grinning teeth.

"You're a horse, not a donkey," Linda told him. She looked tired and bothered, but pretty, too, in her nice pink dress. "Now be careful with that costume, you boys. The Library Service are having Cuts, so we can't afford to replace it if it gets damaged. Here, Charlie, let me hook you up."

Charlie put down his Magic book in a safe place until later, when Duggie Bubbles was due to arrive. There was a great deal of frantic activity going on all around them. Busy helpers were running in and out, and Linda was answering their questions and giving last-minute instructions as she helped Charlie into his back legs. Once inside, he had to hold on to Dodger's waist firmly. He could see very little, although there were some air-holes so he could breathe.

"For heaven's sake don't go walking backwards," Linda warned Dodger sternly, "and give plenty of warning when you're going to stop."

She fixed large notices on either side of them: "Book Bonanza Today!"

They were off, cantering down the passage, with Dodger whinneying realistically and Charlie behind swishing his tail. The Bonanza had officially begun.

Down on the river, the morning was still and calm. A few seagulls rode the water behind the barge, hoping for breakfast. Mr Dix opened the cabin door a few inches and peered round. Then, having made quite sure that he was not being observed, he locked the door carefully behind him and walked on to the deck. He carried a large book casually under one arm, as though he was planning a morning stroll to the library. He hadn't called the police to report the intruders the night before. He had very special reasons of his own for not doing so. Having chased after Trevor a little way, he had given up and returned to the barge in the hope of cornering Ray. But he was too late. Ray had found a rope-ladder hanging down into the water from another barge a little further up-river. Somehow he had managed to heave himself up it, dodge round the gardens, and make off.

Mr Dix crossed the gang-plank and let himself out through the garden gate. He glanced up and down the street a couple of times, then set off at a leisurely pace. As soon as his footsteps had died away round the corner, two faces slid into view at pavement level, looking after him through the railings of a basement area. Trevor was as foxily alert as ever under his clamped-down beret, but Ray was bleary-eyed and sulky.

They climbed up stealthily to street level and hesitated there for a moment. It was very risky to have come back,

but Trevor had decided to take a last desperate chance. Ray had been against it. He had wanted to stay in bed and nurse his aches after the strenuous events of the night before. Being a burglar didn't suit him. He much preferred a more peaceful way of making a living. He and Trevor ran a dubious Antique shop together, where they sold things which might or might not have been stolen by somebody else. They never tried too hard to find out where they'd come from. Trevor knew just where he could sell a valuable drawing if he could get hold of one. But today it was far too dangerous to try to break into the barge again in broad daylight. So Trevor started off up the street after Mr Dix.

"It'll be all up if he sees us this time," said Ray, hobbling after him. "He'll recognize me for sure and you, too, probably. He'll have us arrested."

"Call the police? You must be joking. He doesn't want to have anything to do with the law, any more than we do." Trevor paused on the corner and peeped round. "Nasty questions. Trouble. The last thing he wants."

"What'll we do if we catch up with him?"

"We're *tailing* him. Just keep out of sight and do as I say."

"I think I've done my back in, Trevor. Felt it go as I hit the water last night."

"So it's your back now, is it?" said Trevor unsympathetically. "What I've ever done to deserve such a useless, gutless, witless partner I don't know. I'd have that drawing by now if I was working on my own."

"I wish you were," said Ray.

A huffy silence followed between them. Lurking in and out of doorways, they followed Mr Dix's progress. Once or twice he glanced back over his shoulder but Trevor managed to keep out of sight, bundling Ray with him. When they reached the busy High Street it became easier not to be spotted, although once or twice they nearly lost sight of him amongst the shoppers. Through a street market and down another side-street, they arrived at the main square. Suddenly Mr Dix seemed to disappear. Anxiously Trevor quickened his pace. Forgetting all caution, he craned his neck above the crowd. Ray caught his arm.

"There he is, Trevor," he said, pointing. "On the steps of the hall over there, where all those flags are. Book Bonanza it says. He's going in there!"

"Come on, then," said Trevor.

13 Horsing Around

Mr Dix was paying his entrance money for the Bonanza when Ariadne clanked past. She was so astonished when she saw him that she nearly dropped her banner. For a moment they came face to face, regarding one another. But Mr Dix was not the kind of person to be amused by an outlandish figure in fancy dress. He pushed on past her into the crowded hall.

Ariadne watched him carefully through her tin visor. He began wandering round the exhibition, stopping now and again to idly flip through a book on one of the stands. Children swarmed everywhere, chatting excitedly, devouring books, collecting badges, filling in quizzes and popping balloons. Ariadne started to make her way round the backs of the stands, pretending she was circling the hall with her banner. She was watching his every move. He strolled round casually in the throng, but he kept glancing about, his dark glasses ranging the hall for something. Or somebody. Once or twice he raised his eyes suddenly from a book and nearly caught Ariadne peering at him from behind the display, but she hurried on, flashing her light innocently.

She noticed that he carried a book under his arm. She

couldn't get near enough to read the title. But when a newly-arrived class of primary school children momentarily surrounded Mr Dix and swept him along in their midst, she managed to jostle near enough to read: *Magic for Boys and Girls* by Duggie Bubbles.

"That's odd," said Ariadne to herself, "very odd. Not at all typical. Oh dear, I wish Norman was here."

Charlie, meanwhile, was already feeling hot and tired inside the back legs of the horse. They had been capering up and down the steps of the hall for some time, displaying their notices and trying to attract the crowds. Dodger, quite carried away with his part, was whinneying gaily, browsing in people's shopping baskets for carrots and gnashing his teeth at them. He caused quite a stir. One little girl even timidly offered him a lump of sugar, which Dodger accepted with a great show, tossing his mane and licking his chops. All this was rather boring for Charlie, who felt that his supporting role of back legs offered no such artistic scope. All he had to do was to hold on to Dodger's belt and go wherever he was led, occasionally kicking out his legs. He was just thinking of suggesting that they have a breather and go to see if there was any free orange drink going in the back room, when they were violently cannoned into by Trevor and Ray, who were running up the steps in a great hurry.

Dodger was caught off-balance and fell back on to Charlie. They sat down heavily, Dodger in Charlie's lap. The two men tripped over both of them. Together they all rolled down several steps on to the pavement.

"Hey, mind my ears!" shouted Dodger, forgetting for the moment that he was supposed to be a horse. Charlie was furious. He couldn't see anything. What was more, this was the fourth time he'd been knocked over in the last twenty-four hours. Blindly he fought his way out from the tangle of limbs. At this moment one of the seams on the horse costume gave way under the strain and Charlie's head popped through, about where the saddle ought to have been. Trevor and Ray stumbled to their feet and ran on up the steps without a backward look. The same two men!

"Those two again!" muttered Charlie, scowling. "They seem to be making a hobby of pushing me over. How many more times are they going to try it?"

"Get your head down," Dodger hissed at him. "You're spoiling everything."

Charlie popped back inside and followed obediently after Dodger as he trotted back up the steps and into the hall in the direction of the back room. They had both had enough of being a horse for the moment. It was certainly time for a breather.

"What are those two doing here, anyway?" wondered Charlie aloud as they were sucking up their orange drink. They were both still wearing their horse's legs while a lady helper was kindly doing some running repairs to the torn seam. Dodger had thankfully removed the head, which sat on the table, grinning amongst the general confusion.

"Perhaps they're following you about," Dodger suggested. "Perhaps they've got up a special club to go about pushing you over. Some boys did that to me once in the school playground. It was awful. But me and my gang fought them off in the end."

"But they didn't even know it was me," said Charlie. "And they don't look like the sort of people who'd be interested in Book Bonanzas. When we get into our costume again let's go and find out what they're doing."

14 Mixed Infant

A puppet show was in full swing. Trevor and Ray were stalking the main hall, keeping well to the side among the ornate pillars. They had already spotted Mr Dix who was still loitering rather aimlessly among the stands.

"What's he want to come in here for?" whispered Ray hoarsely. "It's all kids' books in here." Pausing, he pulled one down from a nearby display. "Fairy-tales! I like those. Giants, witches, princesses and that. I always wanted to be a writer of children's stories you know, Trevor. Just look at these lovely pictures!"

He began to turn the pages with interest until Trevor grabbed the book and thrust it back on the shelf.

"Keep watching Dix," he said irritably. "Don't take your eyes off him."

They began to work their way round behind the stands, still trying to keep Mr Dix in view without being seen. Every so often they passed and repassed Ariadne who was still circling in the opposite direction.

"A robot!" cried Ray, turning to look at her with delight. He seemed to have quite forgotten about his bad back. "Look, Trevor, flashing blue light and all. Clever, isn't it?"

"Reminds me too much of a police car," muttered Trevor, pushing him roughly on.

Charlie and Dodger, back again in their horse costume, were hovering behind them in the shadows.

"What are they doing?" whispered Charlie. It was maddening not to be able to see, and to have to rely on Dodger to tell him everything that was going on. Dodger poked his horse's head round a pillar.

"Just walking round. Seem to be looking for somebody."

"Let's follow them."

They set off at a stately pace, daintily picking up their feet. Ariadne, manoeuvring on the other side of the hall, seemed to be making some kind of signals at them, waving her robot arm frantically. But Dodger couldn't understand what she was pointing at.

The puppet show drew to a close, amid noisy applause. Linda's voice came over the loud-speaker, announcing the next event. The Lady Illustrator had arrived and was going to draw some pictures for the younger children in the smaller room off the main hall. There was a general move in that direction. The spaces round the stands suddenly emptied out. Trevor and Ray were dangerously exposed to view, and, what was worse, Mr Dix seemed to be heading straight for them.

"Quick, Ray, he'll see us. Get out of the way," said Trevor.

They shuffled into a crowd of parents and small children who were filing into the smaller room, where an easel had been arranged with a large piece of blank paper pinned to it. The Lady Illustrator was there already, felt pen in hand.

"Now make yourselves comfortable, everybody," called Linda, who was there to introduce her.

Trevor and Ray lowered themselves uneasily on to cushions on the floor among a drove of toddlers. The grown-ups, perched at the back of the room on chairs and tables, shot them an odd look or two, but the Lady Illustrator started off at once with some bright chat. She was large and artistic-looking, dressed in a colourful tent-like garment and hung about with beads. The effect was of an Indian squaw who was accidentally wearing her own wigwam. She asked the children what they would like her to draw. Some of them were too shy to suggest anything, but after some encouragement the braver ones began to call out some ideas.

"Draw a monster!"

"Draw Red Riding Hood!"

"Draw a wolf!"

The Lady Illustrator worked away obligingly, filling  page after page with large felt-pen sketches. Sometimes she paused to answer questions about books and drawing. The children were getting braver and more inventive.

"Draw Rumpelstiltskin!"

"Draw my auntie's budgie!"

"Draw the centre-forward of our team, scoring a lovely goal!"

The Lady Illustrator's hair had begun to escape rather wildly from her bun. The floor was covered with pictures. Ray leant forward with interest. He would have liked to ask her to draw something for him but he knew it would make Trevor cross. A small stir was created at the back of the room as a horse's head appeared inquisitively round the door, but Linda hurried over to it.

"You can't come in here, you two," she whispered. "Go back outside *at once*!"

"What are they doing in there, anyway?" Charlie wanted to know.

"Just Art, that's all," said Dodger.

Now Linda and the Lady Illustrator unrolled a huge piece of paper on the floor. Felt pens were liberally distributed amongst the audience. The Lady Illustrator started to sketch the long shape of a dragon, stretching from head to tail almost the length of the room. Every-

body gathered round and began to join in, filling in the details for themselves. There was a great deal of interested chatter.

"I'm drawing a man with a spear chasing the dragon from behind."

"My man's shooting arrows."

"This is lots and lots of smoke coming out of his mouth . . ."

"And burning flames . . ."

"I'm doing his big pointed teeth."

"Lend us the red a minute, will you?"

"Hang on, I want it for all the dripping blood."

The Lady Illustrator hovered encouragingly, helping the younger ones with a shape here and there. Trevor began to eye the door, shifting restlessly on his cushion. Ray couldn't resist the temptation to pick up a green felt pen and, hoping that Trevor wasn't looking, he carefully began to fill in some neat scales on the dragon's tail.

"We've got to get out of here," muttered Trevor. "For Pete's sake, Ray, stop messing about. We've probably lost Dix by now, and you're acting like a mixed infant."

Ray reluctantly gave up his pen to the little girl next to him, and he and Trevor edged their way towards the door.

Charlie and Dodger were patrolling about outside. Dodger caught sight of them as they slipped out of the door into the main hall. The crowds were denser than ever. Children of all ages, Mums, Dads, Grandpas and Aunties milled happily round the stands, browsing and choosing. Before Trevor and Ray could sight the figure of Mr Dix, there was a commotion over by the main entrance. People were gathering, craning over one another's shoulders. A voice on the loud-speaker announced:

"Your attention, please, everyone. Duggie Bubbles has just arrived! He'll be signing your books at the big stand in the centre of the main hall. Don't miss the Magic Show, which will follow shortly."

Charlie tugged at Dodger's belt.

"Come on, Dodger. Never mind about those two now. We've got to get out of this suit quickly. I want to get my book signed."

15 Smile, Please

The drawing session was over. Willing helpers were clearing up. The Lady Illustrator was being revived with cups of tea. Linda hurried over to welcome Duggie Bubbles and to check for the hundredth time that everything was ready for him on the stand. He was already surrounded by a crowd of children, waving books and bits of paper, and he was signing busily, chatting to reporters from the local paper and flashing porcelain smiles about him, all at the same time.

"Now don't push, children. Just make a little space and wait your turn," said Linda. Organizing a Book Bonanza was even harder work than she had imagined.

Charlie, freed from his role as back legs, shot up to join the queue, clutching his copy of *Magic for Boys and Girls*. Dodger, determined not to be left out of anything, followed close behind. The press of people round Duggie Bubbles was growing all the time and, in spite of Linda's words, there was a certain amount of excited jostling. Charlie found himself being pushed against someone, and nearly fell over for a fifth time with sheer astonishment when he saw who it was: Mr Dix! He turned his dark glasses towards Charlie for a moment, but if he recognized him he had certainly decided to ignore the fact.

"What's *he* doing here?" whispered Dodger from behind. "There seem to be some awfully funny people at this Bonanza."

"*I* don't know. Perhaps he's studying to be a magician, like I am," Charlie whispered back. But he was too busy trying to keep his place in the queue to bother about Mr Dix. He badly wanted to get to Duggie Bubbles and ask him how he did that trick of being tied up in a box and getting out again. He wanted to try it sometime, but he had privately decided not to ask Dodger to be his assistant. Something was bound to go wrong if he did. Mr Dix had somehow managed to push ahead of them. Now he was already thrusting his copy of *Magic for Boys and Girls* into Duggie Bubbles' hands. Charlie, not to be outdone, ducked under his outstretched arm.

"Hold it a minute, Duggie," said a news photographer. "Let's have one of you holding up your books and some of the kids . . . you, with the cap, and you . . . would you mind stepping to one side a moment, sir?"

He pushed Charlie and Dodger into a group with Duggie Bubbles in the centre, holding up two copies of *Magic for Boys and Girls*, one in either hand.

"Let's have a big smile, now!" said the photographer.

The camera flashed. Mr Dix skulked in the background, his jaw set angrily.

"Hey, Charlie, we're going to be in the newspaper!" said Dodger, all agog.

"About that trick, the one where you get shut in the box," Charlie began. "Please can you tell me . . ."

But Duggie Bubbles didn't seem to be listening. He was still smiling and signing, but his face was half turned towards Mr Dix. They exchanged a few quick words over Charlie's head. Then the crowd pressed forward impatiently and Charlie's chance was lost.

"There were lots of things that I wanted to ask him about, and now I'll never find out," Charlie grumbled to Dodger when he found himself pushed out to the edge of the crowd again, with his book under his arm.

"Typical!" commented a voice from behind them. It was Ariadne of course. She was still wearing her robot suit, but she had propped her banner up against a pillar and was watching events from the side of the hall. "There are some fishy things going on at this Bonanza, Charlie, if you ask me. I've been following Mr Dix around for ages but I still can't make out what he's doing here. He certainly doesn't seem much interested in the books."

"And we've been trying to track two *very* fishy characters who keep pushing me over," said Charlie. "Only we've lost them now," he added.

"Pathetic!" said Ariadne. "Oh, dear. I can't think what we ought to do now. It's awfully bad for my brain being inside this robot suit. If only Norman was here."

"He is," said Dodger. "Look, over there."

"Thank *goodness*," said Ariadne with relief. They all hurried over to where Norman was examining a pop-up book with great interest.

"Got off early from work," he told them. "Thought I'd come along and see what's happening. Where's Linda?"

All three children started to talk at once, each telling him something different. But their voices were drowned by another announcement on the loud-speaker:

"The Duggie Bubbles Magic Show will begin in five minutes on the stage at the end of the main hall. Take your places, please."

"Come on, let's try and get near the stage," said Charlie, dragging Norman's arm. "We'll tell you everything later. I want to watch all the tricks from really close up so I can see how he does it."

There was a rush for seats. There weren't enough for everyone. Charlie nimbly threaded his way through the crowd and just managed to bag a place in the second row. Dodger immediately plumped himself down in the row behind him, but Norman and Ariadne were somehow left behind.

"Where are they?" said Charlie, craning his neck. "I hope they don't get left in the standing-room-only."

There was a buzz of excitement all about them. Some helpers were setting up the stage for Duggie Bubbles' act. There was a small table with a fringed cloth, some screens and a trolley with all sorts of strange objects on it. On either side of the stage there were displays with huge posters of Duggie Bubbles' larger-than-life-size smiling face and many copies of *Magic for Boys and Girls*.

"Let's see where he's written his name in your book," said Dodger, leaning over the back of Charlie's seat. Charlie opened his copy at the front page.

"I've been fiddled!" he cried furiously. "This isn't my book! Look, it's got Duggie's signature in it all right, but it hasn't got mine. I wrote it in specially, 'This Book Belongs to Chas. L. G. Moon'. I've got the wrong book!"

"Well, it looks much better than your old one, anyway," said Dodger. "Yours had all that marmalade and tomato ketchup spilt on it. Hey, when's this show going to begin?" He stood up in his seat, trying to catch a glimpse of Duggie Bubbles in the wings.

"But I don't *want* this one," muttered Charlie indignantly, flicking through the pages. "I *liked* my old one. What's this, then?"

He had come across a loose leaf of paper, concealed between two of the pages. It was just smaller than the size of the book, quite thin, and overlaid with a sheet of tissue paper. Charlie folded it back. A face looked up at him that he knew well, a very pretty face, framed with long curly hair: The Stunner.

16 Black Magic

Ariadne had been separated from Norman in the rush
for seats. She was trying to make her way among those
people who were standing at the side of the hall, to get
nearer to the stage, when a burst of applause greeted the
appearance of Duggie Bubbles himself. He launched at
once into a flow of jokes and patter, at the same time
doing some astonishing things with playing-cards, shuffling them with the greatest skill, picking aces out of his
ears, his hair, and what seemed like empty air. He
followed with a rapid succession of tricks with coloured
balls (which appeared from some equally extraordinary
places), and tossed a silk cloth over a transistor, which
was blaring out military marches at full blast, and threw
the whole thing into the air, making the set disappear

abruptly and the music with it. Before
the audience had finished applauding,
he was pouring out all kinds of coloured
liquid into glasses and making those
disappear too. And never once did he
stop smiling and cracking jokes.

Then came the familiar empty top
hat from which he began to pull

yards and yards of multi-coloured
silk handkerchiefs, paper
flowers, strings of sausages, miles
of streamers, and, finally, two snow-
white live doves. One of them strutted,
cooing, across the stage. The other
fluttered up to the rail of one of
the old theatre boxes and perched there,
calmly preening its feathers.

The audience were all intent on
Duggie Bubbles as he started yet another
trick. He was keeping them all laughing.
But Ariadne was looking up. Behind
the curtains of the box she had
caught sight of something. A man's
figure was standing there, half hidden
in the shadows. When he moved slightly,
the glasses gleamed. Mr Dix, like a
Demon King waiting in the wings, was
staring down at the stage.

Ariadne tried to attract Norman's attention. She could see him over the tops of people's heads, standing next to Linda, but she couldn't get near them. Every time she tried to wave, her suit made a noise like a binful of old tin cans.

"I've just got to get out of this thing," said Ariadne to herself. She edged her way over to the exit and set off down the corridor to the small untidy helpers' room behind the stage.

Ariadne was not the only person who had seen Mr Dix up there. Trevor and Ray, in a dark corner beside the display of posters, were still hot on his trail.

"There he is!" whispered Trevor.

"Where?" said Ray, gazing about him.

"Shhhh, shhhh!" said all the people round about.

Trevor was already pushing his way through them towards a side exit.

"I can't think why we're *bothering*," said Ray, lowering his voice to a piercing whisper as he struggled behind. "He's probably flogged that drawing by now."

"*Would* you mind being quiet?" said a lady threateningly.

Up on the stage Duggie Bubbles was saying, "Now, I'm going to ask a member of the audience to step up here. Don't be shy, now—any boy or girl—what about you, young man? Would you come up and give me a hand?"

"He means you," said Dodger, giving Charlie a shove from behind.

"What?" said Charlie, startled.

"That's right," said Duggie. "The young man in the red cap. We've met before this afternoon, haven't we? Bring your book with you."

Bewildered, and clutching the copy of *Magic for Boys and Girls* with The Stunner still between the pages, Charlie found himself being helped up the steps and on to the stage. Beaming, Duggie Bubbles was pumping him by the hand.

"Now, what's your name? Charlie? This is Charlie, everyone! Give him a big hand now!"

Charlie smiled foolishly as everybody clapped, but the clapping soon turned to laughter as, when Duggie released his hand, he found himself holding an egg. It seemed to have appeared out of nowhere. He was even more surprised when Duggie pulled another one out of his left ear. And before he could wonder how it got there Duggie said,

"Would you mind lending me your handkerchief? I've got a shocking cold," and he began to pull one coloured silk handkerchief after another out of Charlie's back pocket.

Charlie stood there with the book under his arm, blinking with amazement. Things were happening too quickly. The events of the last few minutes seemed unreal, as though he had truly been bewitched. Only Dodger's face, open-mouthed, in the audience below, seemed to make sense.

Mr Dix had shrunk back into the shadows of the box. Quietly he opened the door at the back and slipped out. He paused at the top of the flight of stairs which led down to the corridor below, listening. There seemed to be nobody about. Everyone was watching the show. Gales of laughter came from the hall as Duggie Bubbles pulled more and more extraordinary things out of Charlie's pockets. Suddenly Mr Dix heard footsteps running along the corridor and up the stairs towards him. As they drew nearer he heard a voice saying,

"I think I ought to go home, Trevor. Sitting on that floor hasn't done my back any good, you know—"

Trevor and Ray came round the turn in the stairs and they all met face to face. Mr Dix recognized them both instantly. He towered above them, dark with rage.

"You! Following me about, are you? Spying on me, eh? Tried to break into my barge last night, didn't you? Well, I'm going to settle you two, once and for all!"

But Trevor and Ray had already turned in their tracks like lightning and were scrambling back down the stairs the way they had come. With Mr Dix after them, they swerved into the corridor and tore off towards the helpers' room at the other end. Ariadne was just coming out. They cannoned into each other head on.

"Quick, Ray!" gasped Trevor, pushing her roughly out of the way. He wrenched open a small door on his right and both men tumbled down the dark flight of steps which led into the space under the stage. Ariadne flattened herself against the wall as Mr Dix rushed past in hot pursuit. He disappeared after them like an angry ferret down a rabbit-hole.

Ariadne tip-toed to the door and peered after them into the darkness below. The sounds of a struggle had broken out. She could hear them scuffling and blundering about.

"Typical!" she commented under her breath.

Meanwhile, on the stage above, Duggie Bubbles had taken the book from under Charlie's arm and was holding it up to the audience.

"Here it is, folks: *Magic for Boys and Girls*! All the secrets of wizardry and illusion! Let me show you . . ."

Before Charlie could stop him, he began to turn the pages. As he did so clouds of confetti flew out and drifted like snow across the stage.

"There's plenty of good card tricks in here," said Duggie, as, from another opening, he drew out four aces, "but you have to be very careful about taking this magic book up to bed with you at night, you know, Charlie, very, very careful indeed."

Out of the book came a folded piece of paper. Duggie shook it open. It was not, as Charlie had expected, The Stunner, but a huge concertina of black tissue paper on which was painted a grinning skeleton with gangling arms and legs.

The thumps and bumps that were going on under the stage were drowned in applause as Duggie handed the book back to Charlie, and he made his way back to his seat.

"How on earth did he do it?" said Dodger, awe-struck. "I was watching him all the time and I never saw him put all those things in between the pages."

But Charlie didn't answer. He was searching through the book, page by page. Suddenly he leapt to his feet with a wild shout, as though he'd been scalded. The Stunner had disappeared!

"Sit *down*! We can't see!" chorused the children in the row behind.

But Charlie wouldn't sit down. This was all just too much. He felt as though he was going to burst. Scarlet in the face, he stormed back up the steps and on to the stage, stopping Duggie Bubbles dead in mid-patter.

"The drawing! Where's that drawing?" shouted Charlie. He was so furious he felt like a giant. The very boards seemed to be trembling under his feet. The audience, thinking that this was all part of the show, clapped him good-humouredly.

The commotion under the stage was getting louder. The boards were trembling all right, as Trevor and Ray crashed about in the dark beneath, grappling grimly with

Mr Dix. Just then Ray struck out with a wild swinging blow, missed, and fell flat on his face, bringing Mr Dix down with him. Trevor staggered against them, clutching at a wooden lever for support. It gave way. There was a strange clanking noise and a groaning of old boards. A trap-door in the stage above swung open, and Duggie Bubbles disappeared abruptly from view. Charlie found himself alone on the stage, staring down at a heap of wildly waving arms and legs in the pit which had opened at his feet.

17 A Game of Grandmother's Footsteps

The audience loved it. They clapped loudly. It seemed like the perfect ending to a Magic Show for the Magician himself to disappear. This was even better than television.

"Something's gone terribly wrong!" gasped Linda, clutching Norman's arm. Together they hurried out of a side exit and ran to the door which led down under the stage. There they met Ariadne, still peering down the steps with some interest.

"A big fight," she told them briefly, "Mr Dix and two other men. And I think there's someone else in there now, but I can't think how he got there. It's too dark to see who's winning."

The sounds of struggle and terrible oaths which came from below were getting louder and louder. At last one figure broke free and lumbered up the steps. It was Ray. He was wild-eyed, his sleeve was ripped, and he was covered in cobwebs and grime. Closely on his heels followed Trevor, in a similar sorry state. One after another they pushed past the little group at the top of the steps and ran off at full speed in the direction of the main exit. A third figure staggered out after them. Without his

cap or his dark glasses, Mr Dix was almost unrecognizable. He was very nearly bald and his eyes seemed nakedly small and deep-set, like those of an angry gorilla. His teeth were bared in a snarl of rage. He didn't look in the least like his usual self, but, for a split second, Ariadne thought he seemed oddly familiar. He gave them all a furious, lowering look before pursuing Trevor and Ray down the corridor at amazing speed.

"Are you all right, Mr Bubbles?" called Linda anxiously from the top of the steps.

"What do *you* think?" answered a hollow voice from the gloom below.

In the hall above the audience were still applauding, half hoping for an encore. When none was forthcoming they began to drift happily away. It had all been a huge success. They had never expected, when they paid their entrance money, that the Book Bonanza was going to be quite such a lively event as this.

Charlie stood hesitating on the stage, all his anger suddenly deflated. Too many weird things had happened all at once. He felt so bewildered he was ready to cry. He had even begun to wonder if he really had found The Stunner's picture inside that book, or if he'd imagined the whole thing. Dodger scrambled up on the stage to join him.

"That last bit was great, wasn't it?" he said, peering down the trap-door. "I never expected him to do that."

Down below Linda and Norman were helping Duggie Bubbles up the steps and leading him away to the helpers' room at the back of the stage. Luckily he was more or less unhurt. Landing on top of Ray had cushioned his fall. Linda apologized over and over again, and flustered helpers rushed for cups of tea and brandy.

Dodger wandered curiously about the stage. He peered into Duggie Bubbles' top hat and cautiously touched one or two other props, half afraid that some magic might suddenly rise up out of them and take him unawares. But Charlie hadn't the heart to investigate. He had decided in the last half hour that he didn't want to be a conjuror any more. Making magic was altogether too difficult, and, even if you could make it, still harder to control. And being on stage with a real magician hadn't been any fun at all. It had just made him feel foolish. He wandered off across the stage, miserably kicking up some bits of confetti which were still lying there.

"Hey, look, Charlie!" called Dodger. "Here's that skeleton thing that he pulled out of the book!" And he jerked the paper concertina open with a flourish. Some-

thing fell out of it and drifted across the stage, coming to rest at Charlie's feet. He picked it up. Then he let out a yell of triumph.

"It's The Stunner!" he shouted. "I was right! He *did* take it after all!"

"Not that drawing again," said Dodger. "I just can't understand why everyone goes on about that silly old drawing."

All the same, he followed Charlie as he rushed off to the helpers' room to find Norman, waving The Stunner. Linda, Norman and Ariadne were hovering attentively about Duggie Bubbles, who was slumped in an armchair. He wasn't smiling any more. His eyes popped and his jaw hung slackly, making him look more like a discarded ventriloquist's dummy than a magician.

"Here's The Stunner . . ." began Charlie breathlessly. "Got her back . . . found her in my Magic book . . . only it turned out not to be my Magic book after all . . . couldn't tell you, Norman, because then I had to go up on the stage and be magicked at myself . . . and when I got off it again, it wasn't there, you see, and so . . ."

Nobody was listening to this explanation, even if they could have followed half of what Charlie was trying to tell them. They were all staring at The Stunner. Ariadne was the first to recover from her surprise. She took the drawing out of Charlie's hand and looked at it carefully.

"I think it's The Stunner, all right, the real one," she said. "I *am* glad to see her again."

"We've just found it, up on the stage," Charlie explained. "Inside that skeleton thing."

Now they all turned to Duggie Bubbles. His expression was blank. He was the only one among them who had showed no surprise at Charlie's dramatic entrance.

"I never wanted it," he said. "Didn't want anything to do with it. Never saw the wretched thing until today."

"It's Linda's uncle's drawing," said Norman quietly, "and apart from being valuable, it's very precious to him for family reasons. At the moment he still hasn't realized that he's been robbed of it, because there's a clever fake hanging on his wall in its place, put there by Mr Dix. We couldn't tell you, Linda, until after the Bonanza was over. We didn't want to worry you, and anyway, we weren't sure. But now perhaps you'd like to explain, Mr Bubbles, what it's doing here."

Duggie Bubbles' face had lost all its doll-like pink colour. He looked suddenly grey, and years older.

"It'll be the end of my career if this goes any further. I'll be finished if the papers get hold of it . . ." His voice trailed away miserably. They waited. "You see," he said, "Duggie Bubbles is my stage name. My real name's Douglas Dix. Howard—that's Mr Dix—is my older brother."

"I *thought* there was something familiar about him when I saw him without his dark glasses!" said Ariadne.

"I don't see him very often. We've never got on well. He's a lot older than me, and I don't like some of the ways he has of making money," Duggie told them. "Anyway, being seen about with him wouldn't have been very good for my image. But he rang me up out of the blue the other day and said he wanted me to keep something for him. For safety, he said. A small drawing. Said there were some people he didn't trust watching the barge, and he had to get rid of it as soon as possible."

"Why didn't he ring the police?"

"Oh, he'd never do that. He doesn't like to involve the police for, er, personal reasons. I didn't like it at all. But he puts a lot of pressure on. Says he knows things about me that would ruin my career. So I said I'd go down to the barge and collect it from him. Last night, that was. But when I got near to the river there seemed to be a spot of trouble going on. Some sort of fight. So I beat it as fast as I could. You can't afford trouble in show business, you know."

"We were there too," put in Charlie, "I saw you. Do you remember, Norman? And those two men, the ones that kept pushing me over. They were here today, at the Bonanza."

"They must have been the same two who were watching the barge. They must have been after The Stunner too," said Norman.

"Probably," Duggie agreed. "My brother telephoned me again early this morning. Sounded pretty anxious.

Said he was being watched all the time, but that he was going to get to the Book Bonanza somehow—he knew I was making a personal appearance there—and smuggle the drawing to me in a copy of my book. He wanted me to hang on to it for him until the coast was clear."

"So *that's* what Mr Dix was doing at the Bonanza," said Ariadne. "I followed him all afternoon, but I never guessed he had The Stunner inside that book."

"And we were following those two men, who were following Mr Dix . . ." said Charlie.

"Until he turned round and caught them at it. Just like a game of Grandmother's Footsteps!" finished Ariadne.

"I thought I'd let Howard slip me the drawing," Duggie continued, "but I didn't want to have anything to do with stolen goods. I was going to make him give it back, or return it myself if I could find out who it belonged to. I would even have gone to the police, even if he is my brother. But when I got hold of the book, the drawing wasn't inside. It was the wrong copy. They must have got muddled up when the news photographer was taking the picture. We realized that as soon as we looked inside and saw this kid's name."

"Chas. L. G. Moon," Charlie prompted him.

"Howard was furious. I've never seen him in such a rage. He threatened to ruin my act. So I had you up on stage and got it back."

"But how did you do it?" Dodger wanted to know. "I was watching you every second."

But Duggie Bubbles wasn't telling him that.

"I'm a magician, aren't I?" was all he said.

18 Escape!

Trevor and Ray had reached the River Walk, pouring sweat and sobbing for breath, but still running. Twice they had nearly managed to throw Mr Dix off the scent, skidding round corners, dodging down side-roads, running the wrong way up one-way streets, scattering shoppers at every turn. But he had clung on relentlessly. Though he was the older man by far, rage seemed to fire his pace.

"Oooh, my back! My legs! My weak ankles!" cried Ray piteously as he puffed behind Trevor, but Trevor didn't seem to hear. He was making for a small wooden landing-stage which stuck out from the river embankment between two moored barges. A ladder led down to the water, where a small boat, which belonged to one of them, was tied up. Mr Dix was gaining on them rapidly. They scrambled over a low wall, and across somebody's garden, recklessly treading down the plants. They had reached the landing-stage when Mr Dix caught up with them. Trevor was already half-way down the ladder. Ray was hopping about on the platform above. His shoe had come off. A split second before Mr Dix made a grab at him, he picked it up and hurled it. It caught Mr Dix a

stinging blow on the side of his head. He staggered
about, cursing.

"Wait for me, Trevor!" Ray's voice was a high-
pitched scream.

He slithered down the ladder and gave a great leap
into the boat. It rocked dangerously as he landed in it,
nearly capsized, but not quite. It turned round twice,
quite out of control, drifting away from the landing-
stage. They had no oars. Trevor, hunched in the bows,
was paddling with his hands for all he was worth. Ray lay
flat on his back in the bottom of the boat, moaning.

"Paddle, Ray, you daft idiot, for pity's sake, paddle!"
shouted Trevor.

The boat drifted out a little way and seemed to waver
uncertainly. Ray dragged himself up over the side and
flapped a hand hopelessly in the water. His weight listed
the boat over to one side. It spun round once more.
Then, quite suddenly, a swift current caught it and they
were carried out into the main course of the river, away
on the out-going tide.

Mr Dix was forced to stand there and watch them go. He couldn't contain his fury. Lifting his arms to heaven, he let out a wild cry. He shook his fists in the air. He literally capered with rage. But his foot caught against Ray's discarded shoe. He staggered for a moment, then tipped headlong over the edge of the landing-stage into the river below. Great ripples marked his fall. When at last his dripping head emerged from the filthy water, he was just in time to hear Ray's voice, carrying faintly back over the tide,

"This isn't doing my rheumatism any good, you know, Trevor . . ."

19 A Little Celebration

A few days later, a little celebration was about to take place at Uncle Owen Bowen's. His room had been slightly tidied up and the table was laid with all sorts of delicious food: egg sandwiches, sausage rolls, plenty of chocolate biscuits and a big fruit cake with nuts and cherries on top. There was fizzy lemonade and even a bottle of wine for Uncle Owen himself. Linda had taken him for a stroll by the river. This was supposed to be so the children could get everything ready, but it was really so that Norman could have time to return The Stunner to her original frame and rehang her on the wall without Uncle Owen ever knowing the difference.

"But *why* can't we tell him?" Charlie wanted to know. "It was so exciting about Duggie Bubbles disappearing through the stage and me finding her and everything."

"People as old as Mr Bowen aren't as fond of excitement as you are," Norman told him. "They like a more peaceful kind of life. It's all thanks to you we got her back for him, Charlie. And we'd never have found out what was going on here if it hadn't been for you, Ariadne, and Dodger too. But Linda thinks it's better if he never knows about The Stunner being taken from him. It would only upset him. But we'll have to see that he doesn't let her out of his hands again."

"But what about Mr Dix?" asked Charlie.

"Vanished. Scarpered. Completely disappeared. Or so Linda's just been telling me," said Norman, working away busily. "Nobody's seen him since the day of the Bonanza. I think that magician brother of his, Duggie Bubbles, has told him to get out of London quickly, before there's trouble. Or he might have decided for himself that things were getting too hot for him. He must know by now that he's lost all hope of getting The Stunner for himself, and, what's more, we could have the law on him for forgery if he shows his face here again."

"What are you going to do with that copy?" Ariadne wanted to know.

"Put it in a package and post it through the letter-box of his barge, I suppose," answered Norman. "It's all locked up and empty there, Linda says. Only a few empty milk bottles left on the gang-plank." He carefully straightened the real Stunner in her frame on the wall and stood back to admire his handywork. "Lovely, isn't she?" he said, but he was looking over at the door, where Linda had just appeared, rosy-cheeked and looking rather stunning herself, with Uncle Owen following close behind. He beamed with pleasure at the sight of the loaded table.

"A party! How *kind* of you all. I love parties. Used to go to a lot of them at one time. What a wonderful cake! When can we start?"

(263)

As all the chairs were occupied by stacks of paintings, they began at once, without bothering to sit down.

"A very curious thing about Mr Dix," said Uncle Owen, munching away happily. "Nobody can understand why he left so suddenly. Overnight, without a word, not even to me! A neighbour of mine said she saw him running down the River Walk, dripping wet and shouting, but that must be just wild gossip, of course. Extraordinary fellow. But, do you know, the people from the Welfare Service have been round to see me, and they say I can stay here as long as I like! And, I must admit, it's lovely here without Mr Dix. I can paint down by the river whenever I want to now. Quite like old times. Beauty thinks so too, don't you?" He bent down to offer a piece of roll to the old cat who was purring about his legs.

"Linda and I'll decorate the hall for you when we've got some time off, if you like," Norman offered.

"You're too kind, too kind. Do you know, the whole house has changed since Mr Dix went away? Even the smells seem to have disappeared. And I never hear those footsteps overhead at night any more. I really think Lily must be quite at rest at last."

They all looked at The Stunner. A pale rippling light was thrown up from the river on to the wall where she hung. Even Dodger stopped short, with a chocolate biscuit half-way to his mouth, and gazed at her, as though he'd just caught sight of her for the first time.

"I *think* I see why you were making all that fuss," he said at last, through a mouthful of crumbs, "about her being pinch—" but here Charlie nudged him warningly in the ribs with his elbow, "—about her hanging there," he corrected himself quickly. "She does look rather a pretty kind of lady."

"Not half bad," agreed Norman.

"Beautiful," said Ariadne. "I'm so glad she's yours, Mr Bowen."

"She's only mine in a way," said Uncle Owen, filling his glass. "Art belongs to everyone, really, you know. Especially to you young people—to you, Ariadne, my dear, and Charlie and Dodger here. It gets handed on from us older people to you young ones because it *belongs* to you. It's not something chilly or stuck-up or always in a glass case. It changes all the time. And it's not only painting, it's singing and dancing and books and libraries and telling stories and acting plays and getting a good tune out of a musical instrument. It's yours by right, and it's worth sticking up for and never letting anyone take away from you. Because it's the best present you'll ever have."

"Here's to Art, then," said Norman, raising his glass.

"And here's to *you*, Mr Bowen," said Charlie Moon.

ABOUT THE AUTHOR

Shirley Hughes is best known as an author and illustrator of picture books and she has had over two hundred books published since she started writing and illustrating in 1960. She was born near Liverpool and studied art at Liverpool Art School and Ruskin School of Art in Oxford.

Although many of her picture books are for younger children, she thinks it's just as important to have pictures in stories for older readers. She says about her writing, "In conceiving a story, I tend to think in pictures rather than words, and the text tends to develop out of these, like the captions to a silent film."

If you enjoyed the Charlie Moon stories why not try her picture books for older children, such as ENCHANTMENT IN THE GARDEN and STORIES BY FIRELIGHT.